CAPTIVE'S RETURN

THE KYONA CHRONICLES BOOK THREE: A
NOVELLA .

DEBORAH GRACE WHITE

LUMINANT PUBLICATIONS

CAPTIVE'S RETURN

By Deborah Grace White

Forest of Rune
Kynton
Dragon Realm
VAS
Kerr
Montego
Pravat
KYONA
GREAT RIVER
Nérita
Argath
Alezae
MARSHLAND
NORTH L
SOUTH L
BALENOL
BASE TREE
Rebecca P Kааvо

North Wilds
ELLISA
VALORIA
DRAGONCAVE
LOCH ARINE
Arinton
Basal Headlands
Wyvern Islands
Bryford
ANDS
ANDS
Razed's Bastion
Nohl
Jeweled Peaks
Thirl
THORANIA
Logging Camp
Spice Fields

CHAPTER ONE

Scarlett swung her legs over the side of the bed and slid out from under the covers as quietly as she could, trying not to wake her husband. She smiled to herself as Jonan shifted in his sleep, rolling over to unconsciously claim the now empty space where she had been. She didn't know why she was bothering to be stealthy. She had learned during the year they had been married that he slept like the dead.

She dressed quickly, her stance steady despite the rolling of the ship. Three weeks was enough to find her sea legs. She took a moment to survey herself in the tall looking glass bolted to the floor of the state cabin. There was no vanity in her scrutiny, merely a measuring attempt to make sure everything was in order.

She had been told all her life that she was beautiful. Stunningly so, if the reaction of men everywhere was any indication. It was funny to think how much she used to hate being told she was beautiful. Somehow when Jonan said it, she didn't mind at all. She smiled as she remembered their first meeting, how he had flatly refused to compliment her striking appearance, and informed her that he was not so easily impressed. She had respected him for it, but it hadn't stopped her from being irked. Fortunately he had changed his tune since.

And he wasn't the only one. She seemed to remember calling him repulsive. It had been a lie, of course. She had been quite taken with him from the start, although she would never have admitted it at the time. She glanced over at his form, where he still slept solidly on the bed. The insult was no more true now than it had been then.

The year since their wedding had only improved his appearance. His shoulders were broader, his arms, while still lean, were strong and sure. His dark hair was as little inclined to behave as it had always been, but even with the way it flopped over his eyes now, it couldn't hide the handsome features of the face underneath. The scar on his cheek didn't detract from his appeal—it was a reminder of his willingness to take blows for those more vulnerable than him.

She looked back at her own reflection, catching herself still in the act of smiling at her husband's good looks. Her big brown eyes, so similar in shade to her thick hair, curled around her face in the humid air. She had selected a gown of deep blue for their arrival. The color suited her, but she still knew a moment of misgiving as she regarded her reflection. She reminded herself that the bold statement of arriving in Kyona's traditional color was intentional, but she still felt nervous.

She quickly subdued her hair, tying it back into a braid with deft fingers. She had almost forgotten the way the moisture in the air affected her hair. Kyona's climate was so different from that of her homeland.

Before exiting the cabin, she laid out Jonan's appointed outfit prominently on a chair. He would grumble, but she wasn't going to let him get out of wearing the ceremonial garb King Calinnae had insisted on sending with him. She knew Jonan disliked anything official, but she didn't care. She wasn't sure how much protection it would give him to be arriving as an official emissary of the Kyonan king this time, but she wasn't about to waste any possible advantage.

Scarlett felt a small release of tension once she was up on deck. The cabin she shared with Jonan was the largest and most comfortable on the royal vessel, intended for the monarch's use. But after three weeks the enclosed space made her feel claustrophobic.

She picked her way carefully across the deck in the dim pre-dawn light, smiling in response to the respectful greetings she received from the crew members who were already bustling about. Their words might be respectful, but there was no mistaking the admiring way their eyes lingered on her.

In spite of her normal aversion to shallow compliments, on this occasion Scarlett couldn't quite restrain a smile at their reaction. How could she help being glad she was looking well? Marriage agreed with her, and she was hoping those in Balenol would see it when they looked at her. Apparently the sailors had.

She continued across the deck calmly, reaching the edge and placing her hands on the railing. Some women might find it daunting to be the only female on an extended ocean voyage. But Scarlett had never been easily daunted. She was well able to take care of herself, and except for the lingering glances, everyone had treated her with the utmost courtesy. If anything, the men had kept more distance than was necessary, but she suspected that was due to Jonan's protective presence. He tended to glare if anyone got too familiar, and he was stronger than he looked, her husband. Especially when defending someone else against attack.

Not that she had been at risk of attack. She just hoped the same would be true this time tomorrow.

"Almost there, ma'am."

She turned to see one of the ship's crew watching her from nearby, as he coiled up a length of rope.

"Yes," she said softly.

"Does it feel strange to be going home?" he asked curiously.

Home. The word circled disconcertingly around inside Scarlett's head.

"It is strange," she acknowledged, her voice a little rueful. "But Kyona is home now," she added quickly.

"Of course, ma'am," the sailor said respectfully.

"But it will be strange," she repeated softly.

Her conscience tugged at her for dismissing of her former kingdom. She had spoken the truth—she hadn't thought of Balenol as home in months. But still...it was her homeland.

She shivered as she leaned against the railing. After over a year, today she would set foot on Balenan soil again. Strange didn't even begin to cover it. This homecoming was bringing on a bewildering array of emotions.

She didn't elaborate to the sailor, of course. There was no need to hide her reactions away like she used to, but she didn't think she would ever be comfortable talking about her emotions with strangers.

With those close to her, it was a different story. It was amazing how much she had learned to open up over the last year. With Jonan's patient encouragement, she had become almost transparent, at least with him. But the ordeal before her now was sure to test her emotional resilience, and the closer they had sailed to Nohl, the more she had felt herself closing up again. It was the reason she wanted to rise early today, to spend some time alone as they approached their destination.

It wasn't all bad. There were lots of things she had missed about her former home. The food, the warmth, the very familiarity of everything. The lush beauty of the jungle. But the jungle had bad memories, too. She couldn't help but think of the friends she had lost during the drawn out slave rebellion she had helped to found. None of those people remained in Nohl, of course. Every last one of them, except those who had died, had now returned to Kyona.

She loved her life in Raldon, the new settlement in the Forest of Rune near Kyona's capital city. Living there, she was surrounded mainly by former slaves, and she was thriving. Still, she knew she could never fully settle in Kyona until she had faced the demons she had left behind in Balenol.

But how would her birthplace receive her? When she had left so precipitately over a year ago, no one had known of her secret double life as the leader of the infamous slave resistance. Presumably, everyone now knew. She was filled with both longing and dread at the thought of seeing her aunt and cousins again. But thoughts of many others evoked nothing but apprehension.

She sighed as she pictured Jonan, sleeping below. She knew just the look he would get on his face if he knew she was worrying. The one that said he would go down fighting before letting anyone harm her. But the belligerence he displayed any time there was any question about her safety was anything but reassuring. He had matured since they'd first met, but she didn't think fifty years would be long enough to fully banish his recklessness. And his stubbornness was half the reason she was worried, because the truth was that she was more concerned about his safety than her own. When he had left Nohl, he had stowed away on her father's vessel after breaking out of the dungeon, where he had been thrown pending his imminent execution.

In all honesty, Nohl had a lot of reasons not to welcome either one of them.

This was your idea, she reminded herself sternly. *No use getting cold feet now.*

She turned her attention back to the expanse of water before her, and drew in a sharp breath at the sight of the port, distant, but drawing ever closer. She hadn't realized how soon they would make land. She should've gotten up earlier—she had been hoping for more time to collect herself.

She stared out at the water as the crew continued to prepare around her. The rhythm of their well-practiced activities, along with the steady rise and fall of the ocean, lulled her. She thought again about her family as the sun cleared the horizon. Were their emotions as mixed as hers at the prospect of the upcoming reunion? Aunt Mariska would embrace her, literally and metaphorically, she was sure. But Uncle Rupert? Much less certain. And her cousins...well, who knew?

Giles had said in his last letter that he looked forward to seeing her, but it was hard to know if that was just politeness. At least he had assured her the crown was prepared to formally receive them, extending immunity in recognition of their official status as King Calinnae's emissaries. Cal would not have let them come otherwise. And even so, it had been clear to Scarlett that both he and Queen Elnora had felt misgivings as they were seeing the ship off.

She suspected Cal might even have accompanied them himself if Elnora wasn't expecting. But he would never leave his wife at such a time. Even Scarlett felt regretful to be missing so many weeks of her friend's confinement—Elnora would certainly miss her company. But Scarlett knew she'd put this trip off too long as it was.

As lost as she was in her thoughts, she was aware of Jonan's presence before he reached her side. It wasn't just because she was so attuned to her husband. It was also that old habits were not quickly shaken, and her years as a rebel leader had ensured that she was not an easy person to sneak up on.

"Good afternoon," she teased, responding to the slightly grouchy expression that told her he hadn't been ready to wake up.

He grinned easily, nudging her with an elbow in half-hearted retaliation. "I didn't sleep that late. The sun's barely up."

She looked him up and down and sighed at the rumpled state of his hair. "Didn't you look at your reflection?" she asked. "You do realize we're about to land, and we're supposed to be making a good impression, right? Don't forget, we're representing—"

"Representing the Kyonan crown, yeah, yeah, I know," yawned Jonan. "I already endured this speech from Cal's insufferable master of protocol. If you make me listen to it again, I'll push you overboard."

"I'd like to see you try," she grinned.

He brightened instantly at the challenge, taking a step toward her with a martial light in his eye, but she fended him off, laughing.

"Show some respect for the dress. I didn't bring another one in Kyonan blue, so no dunking me in the ocean until after we've been officially welcomed."

"The color is very nice on you," Jonan commented, looking her up and down properly. "But that's not saying much, because everything is."

She smiled. "It's nice on you, too."

He grunted, unimpressed. "I feel ridiculous. Why Cal insisted on dressing me up like some kind of diplomat I have no idea."

"You have every idea," contradicted Scarlett firmly. "So stop complaining."

"I'm not complaining," Jo protested. "I'm wearing it, aren't I?"

He glanced down his person. "Why should I have looked at my reflection, anyway? Did I put it on backward?"

"You're hopeless," she laughed. He still looked confused, so she nodded at his head. "Your hair. It looks like a bird made a nest in it." She stepped forward as she spoke, running her hands carefully through the unruly mess, bringing it into order.

Jo made a noise of contentment, accompanied by a cheeky grin, and she narrowed her eyes suspiciously.

"Did you mess it up on purpose?"

"Of course not," he said innocently. "Isn't a man allowed to enjoy it when his wife runs her hands through his hair?"

She stepped back, satisfied with her efforts, and met his eye. His expression made her heart speed up a little. She tried to frown, but his knowing smile told her he wasn't fooled. That was the trouble with being transparent instead of emotionally inexpressive. He knew exactly what effect he had on her.

"Stop looking at me like that," she scolded him.

"Why?" he asked, tucking an errant strand of hair behind her ear. Her skin tingled where he had brushed it. She kept waiting for the thrill of nearness to fade, but it hadn't happened yet.

"Because we're in a public place," she said smilingly, and he chuckled.

"How long have you been out here, anyway?" Jonan asked. "You should have woken me up."

She turned away from him, looking toward shore. "Not that long. I just wanted a minute to gather my thoughts."

Jonan followed her gaze, seeming to realize for the first time just how close they were to land. He turned his full attention back to her, resting a hand gently on the side of her neck. He watched her silently for a long moment, and eventually the weight of his gaze compelled her to look up at him. It was one of the things she loved about Jonan—when he gave her his attention, it was undivided. He had seen her true self through all her facades even back when she had hardly known herself, and he hadn't stopped really seeing her since.

"Are you nervous?" he asked quietly.

She started to shake her head, but halfway through the gesture she stopped herself. Who was she fooling? She nodded, a lump forming in her throat at the understanding look in his eyes. Without warning, she turned toward him and buried her face in his chest. He put his arms around her, the gesture comfortable and familiar.

"We don't have to do this, you know. We can still turn the ship around. If you don't want to go, just say the word, and we'll go back home."

She drew back, chuckling weakly as she tried to collect herself. "And I'm sure the crew would have no objection to adding three weeks to the voyage without even stopping to re-provision the ship."

"We could detour to Thorania first," Jonan countered, his expression still serious.

She shook her head. "I need to do this, Jo," she said softly. "Or I'll feel like a coward all my life." He didn't answer, his brow furrowed as he continued to search her features with his clear gaze. She reached out and smoothed the crease between his eyes with her thumb. "You, on the other hand, don't have to prove anything. Maybe restocking in Thorania is a good idea. You could go with the ship—"

"Don't start this again, Scarlett," Jonan cut in. "We've been through this. I go where you go."

"But I don't want to put you in a difficult position," she said, her tone showing her anxiety in spite of herself. "I know you didn't want to come—"

"Don't be ridiculous," said her husband, his tone uncompromising. "It's not that I didn't want to come, it's that I don't want you to put yourself in danger. And if you think for a moment that I'm going to hang back and leave you to face that danger alone—"

"I'm not in danger, Jo," interrupted Scarlett. "Giles said I'll be safe. He's persuaded the crown to look the other way in regards to my past...activities, given that we're coming with King Calinnae's goodwill. The potential for a trade deal with Kyona is much more important for Balenol than punishing me for something that's over and done with now. You know all this. I showed you Giles's letter."

"You showed me part of his letter," Jo corrected. "You were pretty determined for me not to see the second page."

She stilled, looking up at him ruefully. So he had caught that, had he? She hadn't been as subtle as she had thought. The twinkle in his eyes told her that he knew he had caught her out.

"It was nothing about my safety," she said quickly, and Jo chuckled.

"No, I imagine it was your cousin's candid opinion of your husband," he said cheerfully, and she sighed. Sometimes he was a little too astute. "You're adorable Scarlett," he continued affectionately. "Do you really think I've been married to you for a year without learning to tell when you're hiding something?"

"Almost," she said.

"What?"

"Almost a year. Our anniversary isn't until tomorrow."

Jonan gave her a look. "Believe it or not, I do actually know that. Now don't change the subject. Did Giles actually threaten me, or just express his disapproval of your choice of husband?"

"What? Of course he didn't threaten you!" responded Scarlett, startled. "He wouldn't do that." She narrowed her eyes at him. "You thought he did, and you still insisted on coming with me?"

"Of course I did," said Jonan shortly. His expression softened as he took in her frown, and he pulled her against him again. "What's the point of marrying you if I don't have the right to protect you, Scarlett? Besides." He spoke lightly, trying to sound nonchalant. But pressed against him as she was, she could feel his sudden tension. "I don't want to be on the other side of the ocean while all your royal relations try to talk you out of returning to me. Much better if I'm on hand so you can see my rugged good looks and remember why you married me."

She pulled back, frowning. "Are you truly worried about that? Do you think I could be talked out of coming home to you? You should have more faith in me, Jonan." She echoed his own words. "What's the point of marrying you if I still have to convince you or anyone else that we belong together? I'm your wife. No one's going to try to prevent me going back to Kyona with you. Isn't that the whole reason we waited until we were married before coming back here?"

Jonan met her searching gaze but didn't immediately respond. She had expected him to apologize for doubting her, but he didn't. There was a hardness in his eyes that she didn't like.

"I hope you're right about that," he said eventually. "But can you really look me in the eye and tell me that your family, Giles for example, approves of me, or your decision to marry me?"

She looked away quickly, and the slight tightening of his hands where they rested on her shoulders told her that she had proved his point.

"It's complicated," she said, her voice pleading. "Don't be too hard on them."

"It doesn't seem complicated to me," he answered, his voice still hard.

She sighed. She wanted so much for Jonan and her family to think well of each other, but she had accepted that it was unlikely, to say the least.

"My Lord, My Lady? It's time to begin final preparations for our arrival."

"For the hundredth time, we're not a lord and lady." Jonan scowled at the crew member as he spoke, and Scarlett sighed again. The last thing she had wanted was to put Jonan in a belligerent mood right before they landed.

"Thank you," she said softly to the man, quelling her husband with a look. "We will make ourselves ready."

The man bobbed his head awkwardly and walked away, shooting an uncertain look at Jonan, who was still glowering.

"I suppose I'll have to get used to all that rubbish," Jo said when they were alone again. "Everyone in Nohl will be calling you 'My Lady' out of habit."

She shrugged. "I suppose so. But Jonan," she stared him down until he reluctantly met her gaze, "don't let them get in your head. You know I don't care about any of that. I've never once missed being a lady. I love being married to you, and I love the life we have. Don't let anyone make you forget that."

His face softened instantly, and with his usual disregard for conventions, he leaned in and gave her a quick kiss. Strictly speaking it wasn't really appropriate on the deck of the ship, but she returned the gesture uncomplainingly. She could sense that he needed reassurance, and truth be told she wanted the comfort of his touch as well. She wasn't sure how difficult the coming encounter would be, but she wanted to know he was at her side, emotionally as well as physically.

"I'm sorry for getting angry," he whispered, leaning his forehead against hers. "I'm just afraid of losing you."

"You're not going to lose me," she said firmly, and he straightened, his voice becoming determined.

"I know. And you don't need to be nervous, because I won't let any harm come to you. They'll have to kill me first."

"Oh, Jo," she said, exasperated. "It's exactly that attitude that makes me nervous. Just please try not to provoke anyone powerful. For Cal's sake as much as mine!"

"I make no promises," he said, but his eyes once again held laughter. Scarlett turned away with a rueful smile, satisfied that his good humor had returned.

CHAPTER TWO

The two of them remained on deck as the ship was docked and the gangplank lowered. Scarlett's period of quiet reflection had not quite gone as planned, and she felt anything but ready to disembark.

Apparently her husband didn't share her reluctance. Jonan was clearly impatient as the captain went forward to meet with a Balenan man who waited on the quay. Scarlett couldn't help but notice that the man looked very ill-at-ease, his body language showing clearly that he wanted to be elsewhere. And he wasn't the only one. Even from a distance, she could see the frown growing on the captain's brow as he listened. After a moment, he made his way back on board, heading straight for them.

"What's the hold up?" asked Jonan before the man could speak.

"We docked more quickly than they expected," said the captain, still frowning. "The welcome delegation isn't here yet, but they're on their way."

"Good to know," said Jonan cheerfully, starting toward the gangplank.

"Wait," said the captain quickly. "They've requested that you wait on board until their arrival."

"I'm sure they have," said Jonan, unimpressed. "But without meaning to offend you, Captain, I've had more than enough of your ship over the last three weeks. I would like to feel the ground beneath my feet again."

Forestalling further argument, Jonan leaped lightly onto the gangplank and strolled down onto the quay. With an apologetic grimace in the captain's direction, Scarlett followed. The Balenan envoy looked aghast, but didn't actually attempt to stop them as they walked the length of the quay, toward the river that ran through the city of Nohl.

"It feels weird to be back, doesn't it?" asked Jonan, grasping her hand and twining his fingers through hers. He gave her a sideways look. "Are you all right?"

"It does feel weird," she acknowledged. "I'm fine, just...the captain seemed worried, don't you think? Maybe we should have waited on the ship as requested."

"Nonsense," said Jo briskly. "Why shouldn't we stretch our legs? We won't go far. They can as easily welcome us on the quay as on the ship."

Scarlett nodded, but she felt uneasy, some instinct that she couldn't articulate warning her that something was amiss. They had reached the end of the wharf by now, and she looked instinctively toward the castle neighborhood. It was silly, because she knew she wouldn't be able to see it from this distance. All she could see was the row of homes, more hovels than houses, that lined the edge of the water.

The dockside area was one of the poorest neighborhoods in Nohl, and she had never had occasion to spend much time there. Her eyes were drawn to a small child, playing alone on the street with a wooden ball. He was filthy, his clothes ragged and too large for him, and his feet bare. As she watched, the child spun the ball away from him with unintended force, a cry leaving his mouth as it rolled toward the water.

Jonan had also seen, and he stepped forward quickly to intercept the ball.

"Here you go," he said, holding it out to the boy with a grin.

The boy received it cheerfully. "Thanks, mister."

"No problem," said Jonan easily. Scarlett smiled in spite of her unease. It was another thing she had discovered about Jonan over the year they had been married. He was very good with children.

"Who're you?" Her husband had apparently captured the little boy's interest. "You just get offa that big ship over there?"

Jonan nodded, but before he could say another word, a woman appeared from a nearby house, racing forward to snatch up the boy as if he was under attack.

"What you doin', talkin' to strangers?" she said, her voice shrill and unpleasant. Her appearance was little better than that of her son, her clothes dirty and a prominent tooth missing. She barely glanced at Scarlett, her gaze passing to Jonan. She sucked in a quick breath as she looked him up and down. Then she suddenly spat on the ground at his feet, her face twisting in fury.

"Kyonan," she snarled. Without another word, the woman turned and hurried back into her home, the child still bundled in her arms.

Jonan turned to Scarlett, his face uncharacteristically uncertain. "Is it just me, or did that feel different, like things have changed?"

Scarlett's voice was grim. "It's not just you." Jonan was right—the people of Nohl had always been scornful and belittling of Kyonans. But this anger was new. "I don't like it, Jo," she said, making no effort to hide her unease. "I think you should get back on the ship."

His face said plainly that he wasn't going to cooperate, but he had no opportunity to actually answer her. The sound of approaching feet caught both their attention, and they turned to see a squadron of guards, dressed in royal livery, marching at a smart pace toward the quay. The leader caught sight of them, and pulled the squadron to a halt with a gesture.

As the man strode up to them, Scarlett and Jonan exchanged a look of confusion. There were no officials with the guards. A squadron was a strange welcoming party for visiting dignitaries. Was Nohl so unsafe now that they needed an armed escort to reach the castle? A carriage rumbled into view behind the squadron, and Scarlett figured that must be it.

Jonan stepped slightly in front of Scarlett as the man reached them, the protective gesture instinctive. But it seemed she wasn't the one who needed protection.

"Are you Jonan?" the guard barked, and Scarlett bristled at his aggressive tone.

"Yes," said Jonan, matching the man's glare. "What do you want?"

The guard nodded, and two of his fellows stepped forward smartly, clearly intending to seize Jonan.

"What do you think you're doing?!" demanded Scarlett, pushing forward to stand between Jonan and the guards. "How dare you offer us violence?"

"Step aside, Lady Wrendal," said the chief guard gruffly. "This doesn't concern you."

"That's not her name," growled Jonan, at the same time as Scarlett said, "Doesn't concern me? You're attacking my husband, and you say it doesn't concern me?"

"Our orders are to convey you to the castle, My Lady," said the guard stubbornly. "But we're to take the Kyonan," he jerked his head toward Jonan, "to the dungeons."

"Well, your orders are outrageous!" protested Scarlett, assuming a commanding tone in an attempt to hide the panic rising inside her. "We're here as official representatives of King Calinnae of Kyona, and I have been given personal assurance from His Highness Prince Giles that we will be received accordingly!"

"Prince Giles is the one who gave our orders, My Lady," said the guard, a hint of amusement in his voice.

"He—what?" Scarlett felt her mouth drop open, and the guards took advantage of her momentary distraction to seize Jonan by the arms. "Wait!" she cried, but they ignored her.

Her eyes flicked to her husband, and she felt a cold rush pass over her at the hard, almost sneering look on his face as he continued to glare down the guard. Unlike her, he didn't look the least bit surprised, and the sight galled her. She had been so sure she could trust Giles, but it looked like Jonan had been right after all.

"This is absolutely unacceptable!" she blustered, grabbing the arm of one of the guards who had seized Jonan, and trying unsuccessfully to pry his hand off.

"It's fine, Scarlett," said Jonan, his voice resigned. "Did we really think I'd be welcomed into any other part of the castle? As I recall, the dungeons are really quite homey, if you can discount the rats."

"No, it's not fine!" she cried. "You're not going to the dungeons! This is ridiculous."

"Ridiculous or not, the Kyonan is going to the dungeons," said the chief guard, his voice unyielding.

"His name is Jonan!" Scarlett snapped. "And he happens to be my husband." She took a deep breath, mastering herself. "That being the case, I can only imagine we are to be accommodated together. So if he's going to the dungeons, so am I."

"I don't think so," said Jonan flatly.

She glared at him. "I wasn't asking your permission."

"That's not possible, My Lady," said the chief guard coldly.

"Stop calling me that," she snapped, stepping forward to align herself with Jonan. The guard didn't argue with her, but at another nod from him, one of his underlings stepped forward and grabbed her arm, pulling her roughly away from Jonan and toward the waiting carriage.

At once Jonan's languid air disappeared. "Don't touch her!" he cried, his voice sharp. "Get your hands off my wife!" He began to struggle violently against the two guards holding him, and Scarlett gasped when he received a blow to the stomach for his pains.

"What are you going to do about it, Kyonan?" one of the guards jeered.

Jonan had momentarily doubled over in pain, but he straightened in an instant, his voice strong, even though he was clearly winded.

"You'll find out if you touch her again."

One of the guards cracked his knuckles menacingly, and Scarlett's anger was suddenly eclipsed by fear. These men were in earnest, and if things continued on their current course, Jonan was going to get himself killed.

"Enough," she said crisply. "This whole situation is an outrage. I will go with you to the castle and speak to the prince myself. Don't think your unnecessary violence will be forgotten once this mistake has been cleared up."

She glared at each guard in turn, as though memorizing their faces, trying to make them believe she had the power to carry out her threat. Her demeanor showed no hint of it, but she was rattled by the way they sneered back at her, with no sign of alarm on their faces.

A guard stepped forward to escort her, but at her glare he didn't actually touch her. Before she turned toward the carriage, Scarlett met Jonan's eyes, and he gave her a slight nod.

I'll be fine, the gesture clearly said, but Scarlett could feel no such confidence. She knew that he had read her distress and was swallowing whatever fear or anger he might be feeling in an attempt to reassure her.

The thought made her throat constrict. A lesser man would remind her that he had predicted this, but as always, he only cared about protecting her. He hadn't wanted to come here, hadn't wanted her to leave the safety of their home. They had come because she insisted on it. If anything happened to him now, it would be her fault.

She tried not to let her fear show as she climbed into the carriage. As it began to move, and she twisted around to peer through the back window, she could only be thankful that no one else was inside with her. Because her veneer of calm couldn't quite withstand the sight of her husband being bound like a criminal and roughly thrown into the back of a nearby cart.

CHAPTER THREE

The journey to the castle felt interminable, although it couldn't have been more than twenty minutes. Scarlett's mind was full of her fear for Jonan, but even so, she couldn't help watching out the window of the carriage as the familiar streets rolled past.

And yet not so familiar. Although she had lived in Nohl all her life before the last year, she felt like she was looking at an unknown landscape. The buildings and streets were much the same, she supposed. But the people were not. She knew that the dockside district was a poor area, and she had not been surprised by the state of the little boy who had been playing with the ball.

But she was surprised to see similar poverty stretching far beyond the docks. And it wasn't just the physical state of the people she saw out her small window. There was something else —a defeated look in their eyes. And, difficult to pinpoint but impossible to miss, a general sense of anger, simmering just below the surface. There was also something missing, but it took her a while to identify what it was.

The slaves. They had always been a regular part of the city's traffic before, shuffling along with eyes downcast. But now there was not a single Kyonan to be seen. Scarlett remembered the reaction of the woman at the quay, and her chest tightened with anxiety as she realized all over again just how conspicuous her husband was here in Nohl now.

But her discomfort was not merely related to Jonan's well-being. Of course the loss of the slave labor that had carried Balenol's economy for centuries would have had an effect on the affluence of her home city. And she knew that it wasn't right for the people of Nohl to build their wealth on the oppression of the Kyonans. That belief was what had driven her to start the resistance. But still...it wrenched her heart to see the deterioration of the city, and the suffering of its people.

She knew what Jonan would say in response to such thoughts. He would have no sympathy for the people who had stood by and allowed the slave trade to flourish. But as much as she had thrown in her lot with the Kyonans, she was still a Balenan born and bred. She couldn't dismiss her entire kingdom so quickly. She didn't take any delight in her isolation and exile from her own people. It was an inevitable but regrettable effect of the decision she had made long ago.

Not that she regretted the decision, or would change it. But it would always grieve her to be so severed from her own people, and she didn't think Jonan would ever really understand that. The thought made her heart ache.

But no. Here she was, thinking that Jonan was too hard on her countrymen, when at this very moment, he was bound and being hauled to the castle by the same authorities who had given their word he would be peacefully received. She felt her anger at Giles returning full force. Was it any wonder Jonan thought so poorly of her people when they behaved with so little integrity?

She was still in the grip of this galvanizing anger when the carriage came to a stop in the castle courtyard. Without waiting for any sign from her armed escort, she leaped lightly out of the vehicle and swept into the castle's entryway, her air of dignified assurance daring anyone to question her.

She had turned toward the royal wing, the guards who had followed her from the docks hurrying to catch up with her, when she heard a familiar voice.

"Scarlett! You're here already. Welcome."

"Welcome?" She felt her blood boil as she turned to face the attractive young man hurrying down the staircase toward her. "How dare you say 'welcome' to me? How *could* you, Giles?" She glared up at him, making no attempt to keep her voice down. "How could you *dare*?"

Her cousin's face tightened at her words, in a way she knew signified anger, although he was too well-mannered to express it openly. She knew that nothing would annoy him more than if she were to cause an embarrassing scene in front of the various servants who milled around the entranceway. It was tempting to do it, just to test his restraint, but she had no more desire than he did to be the subject of idle gossip.

"You must be tired from your journey, and in need of refreshment," Giles said, the words tight and clipped. Of course he would refuse to even acknowledge her accusation. "Come into my mother's receiving room. She is eager to see you."

Scarlett had been about to hotly retort that she didn't want refreshments, she wanted her husband released, but Giles's mention of her Aunt Mariska made her waver. She did want to see the woman who had been a mother to her all her life. She wanted to see her desperately.

After a moment's hesitation, she gave a tight nod, continuing to glare at Giles so that he would know she wasn't happy about it. Her behavior was a far cry from the carefully controlled demeanor of the haughty Lady Wrendal, but she didn't care. She had no desire to maintain that persona.

She swept past Giles and up the stairs, leading the way to her aunt's rooms. She wanted to remind herself as much as everyone else that she knew her way around here, and was not going to tolerate being treated like an outsider.

She knew a moment's hesitation when she reached her aunt's door. What would Aunt Mariska really think of all Scarlett had done? But there was an interested servant passing by, and Scarlett didn't want to show any uncertainty. She knocked and confidently entered. Giles followed behind her.

"Scarlett! My child! You've returned to us!" Scarlett could hear the tears in Aunt Mariska's voice, and her own eyes suddenly stung as she threw herself forward and into her aunt's arms. They closed around her, and a familiar scent settled over her. How could she have doubted her reception?

"Aunt Mariska!" she said, her voice shaky. "I've missed you."

"I know, my darling, I've missed you too," her aunt soothed, stroking her hair as if she was still a child. And indeed, she felt suddenly like a child again, with no problems too big for her beloved aunt to fix with a smile and a kind word.

If only that were true. She drew back, turning to face Giles, who had shut the door behind him.

"How could you do this, Giles?" she demanded, her eyes and voice hardening. "How could you betray me like this?"

"There's no need to be so dramatic, Scarlett," her cousin said waspishly. "I haven't done anything of the kind. On the contrary, I'm trying to protect you."

"I don't see how having my husband thrown in the dungeons can be considered protecting me," Scarlett said incredulously.

"That wasn't my doing," said Giles quickly.

She raised an eyebrow. "Really? The royal guards who

arrested him said otherwise. Or were they lying when they said they were acting on your orders?"

Giles frowned at her accusatory tone, but at least he had the grace to look uncomfortable. "No, they weren't lying," he admitted. "I did order them to apprehend Jonan and escort him to the dungeons. But I acted for the best."

"For the best?" Scarlett demanded furiously. "Jonan predicted something like this, but I never believed you capable of treachery. It seems he was right all along!"

Aunt Mariska laid a hand on Scarlett's arm. Scarlett was shaking with anger, and it was all she could do to stop herself from throwing it off.

"Hear him out, Scarlett," the older woman said gently. "I understand why you're angry, but he's trying to help you."

"You have a strange idea of what will help," said Scarlett, pain shooting through her at the realization that her aunt was complicit in Giles's treatment of Jonan. "I know you never liked Jonan, Giles, but I never suspected you of duplicity. You personally assured me that we would be received peacefully."

"And at the time I wrote it, I had every reason to believe you would be," Giles shot back. "But things have changed since then. And whatever you may think of me, I've been scrambling for a way to protect you ever since!"

"What things?" demanded Scarlett. "And what are you trying to protect me from that could be helped by imprisoning Jonan?" Her voice turned to steel. "If you think I'm in danger from him, then—"

"No, I don't think that, not exactly," Giles cut her off. But he spoke carefully, and she was anything but mollified.

"Not exactly?" she repeated, her voice growing dangerously quiet. "What does that mean?"

Giles sighed. "It means that I don't think he intends you any harm, but harm is likely to come to you through him anyway."

He turned away from her. "The people are suffering, Scarlett. And they're angry. Things have been hard this last year, harder than they've been in a very long time. And people want someone to blame."

"Maybe they can blame our ancestors who built our economy on such a despicable foundation, so that when the slaves finally received justice, it put our country at risk of collapse."

She tried to speak in the same hard voice, but even to her own ears, her words lacked conviction. She had seen the suffering and the anger herself, just in the short ride to the castle. And as much as she tried to keep it at bay, she could feel the old familiar guilt creeping back in. The guilt that used to eat at her every time she thought about what her family would think if they knew about her secret double life.

"Perhaps that's who we should blame," said Giles heavily. "But people who are long dead don't make a satisfying scapegoat, do they? We can't exactly put their necks under the blade to satisfy the people's bloodlust."

A cold chill ran over Scarlett. "If you're trying," she choked out, "to put Jonan's neck there instead—"

"I'm trying," Giles snapped, with something less than his usual princely dignity, "to keep your neck from being put there. If you would think about something other than your precious Jonan for one minute, you would realize that you are just as notable—and just as hated—a figure as he is." He paused, taking a deep breath and calming his tone with an obvious effort. "Or didn't you know that everyone is now aware of your... clandestine activities back when you lived here?"

Scarlett had gone still at his words, and she spoke quietly, keeping her voice steady with difficulty. "I assumed that everyone would know. That's why I asked you whether it was safe for us to come here."

Her eyes fell on her aunt, taking in the tentative look that had come over her face.

"We...we weren't entirely sure what to...that is, I know that these stories can often grow in the telling. Did...did you really lead the whole resistance, Scarlett?"

Scarlett took a deep breath. She had been expecting this moment. So many times she had both dreaded and longed for a time when she could tell her aunt and her cousin the truth. She should have fought Jonan harder about him coming on this trip, but the truth was she had desperately wanted him by her side when this moment came. And now she was alone anyway.

"Yes, Aunt Mariska," she said quietly. "I did."

Giles drew in a sharp breath. "And you accuse me of duplicity?"

"Giles," said Aunt Mariska warningly, but he ignored her.

"You have the temerity to storm in here, outraged, as if you're the one who's been wronged? How could you do it to us, Scarlett? I always knew you were sympathetic toward the Kyonans, but I never dreamed you would go so far. What form did it take? I suppose you used your position, your relationship to your father, your relationship to *us*, to learn sensitive information about what would hurt us most. Did you pass that information on to them? The rumors are that you did more than just give information, that you got your own hands dirty too. What did you do, disguise yourself and attack with the guerrilla fighters in the jungle? Did you kill people, Scarlett? Our people?"

Scarlett flinched at the harshness of Giles's tone, but she waited silently for him to get it all out before she spoke.

"Yes," she said simply. "To all of that."

CHAPTER FOUR

In spite of herself, Scarlett looked at her aunt, and saw that even she looked shocked, her face unusually pale. Giles's face was frozen, so Scarlett hurried on before she could lose her nerve.

"And even though I took no pleasure in it, in any of it, I can't say that I regret it."

Giles once again turned away from her, but not quickly enough to hide the pain in his features. The betrayal she saw in his eyes made her feel like a knife was being twisted in her gut.

"I've been defending you," he said quietly. "But it seems you really are guilty of treason after all. You're like a sister to me, Scarlett. I didn't want to believe it of you."

"I'm sorry Giles," she said, and the anguish in her voice seemed to catch his attention. He turned slowly back toward her. "I really am sorry. I hated lying to you. I didn't want to harm Balenol, or the crown, and especially not you. But things couldn't go on how they were. The slave trade was heinous. I tried a more peaceful approach, but no one would listen."

"I'm not saying things were perfect," said Giles, his voice

once again hard. "But I hardly think that justified turning on your own people. You've admitted yourself that you killed people! You think that kind of violence was justified?"

"Do you think I liked the violence?" Scarlett demanded, starting to get angry herself. "I hated it! I hated all of it! The violence toward the slaves, the fighting in the jungle, the whippings, the riots, the beheadings, all of it!" Her chest was heaving, and she glowered back at him. "So you think things weren't quite perfect, Giles? What delusion are you living in? You remember when my father moved to Nohl and made me move in with him?"

"I—yes, of course I remember," said Giles, thrown by the unexpected question.

"And do you remember that I didn't want to go, and didn't like living in his house?"

"Yes," said Giles cautiously, as if fearing a trap.

"Almost four years I lived with him," said Scarlett, glaring her cousin down. "Maybe if you'd lived with him that long, you would've started a resistance too. Not that it took me four years. Within the first week I knew that I couldn't go on as I was. Do you know what I witnessed three days after moving in with him?"

She waited, but neither of her listeners spoke, both watching her warily.

"A new slave had just arrived, a young girl. I don't know what she was called. It wasn't until later that I started making the effort to learn their names. Like all of us, I was raised not to think of them as human, after all." She made no effort to soften her words. Her aunt gave a barely perceptible flinch, and even Giles looked uncomfortable.

"Well, she wasn't quite up to scratch, not for the great Lord Wrendal. On my third morning in his house, she ruined his eggs. Apparently it was the third time, and that was one too many. She'd been warned, he said, what would happen if she did it again. So he beat her, mercilessly, right in front of me. She was maybe twelve years old. He beat her so brutally that she died the next day."

Scarlett shrugged, the horror of that moment as fresh as if she was still fourteen and innocent. "I was with him when her death was reported to him. He didn't blink, just said that there were plenty more where she came from, and he hoped the next one would know how to cook eggs better."

Scarlett paused. The silence in the room was absolute, both her aunt and her cousin completely still. Scarlett turned her face slightly to the side, shame washing over her as she continued.

"And I did nothing. I sat there while he beat her, and I didn't say a word. I could see that she couldn't take it, but I was too afraid, too cowardly, to intervene. I learned later of course how to intervene without seeming to, how to manipulate him and direct him without him knowing it."

She shook her head. "I wish I could say that it was an isolated incident, but it wasn't. It was absolutely normal in my father's house. And that wasn't even the worst of it. You probably never even noticed, but we had hardly any female slaves. I made sure of it. I used every trick I could think of to have them assigned elsewhere. I knew that in the castle, for example, slaves were treated much better than they were at my father's house. His soldiers were always hanging around, and the things they used to do to the girls…"

She covered her face with her hand in an involuntary movement. After a moment, she took a deep breath, mastering herself. "Bonnie was different," she said, her voice stronger. "She was tough, and she was almost always with me. If she needed to, she could hide in my rooms, and not even Father's lackeys would dare to go in there."

She looked back at Giles and Aunt Mariska and saw that they were held spellbound by her words. Her aunt had tears in her eyes, and Giles was watching her with a very serious expression on his face.

"Why didn't you tell us all this at the time?" he asked, his voice no longer angry.

Scarlett made a dismissive noise. "I went to Uncle Rupert after my father beat that poor girl to death. I told him what had happened and begged him to let me come back to live at the castle. He agreed that it was 'most unfortunate' that the child hadn't recovered from her punishment. But he said that my father had the right to discipline his slaves as he saw fit, and that he had the right to decide where his daughter would live, and that it would be inappropriate for my uncle to intervene in either matter."

"I never knew that you had spoken to him," whispered Aunt Mariska. "Your uncle didn't tell me."

Scarlett shrugged. "I imagine it was a conversation of little consequence to him. But for me…it changed my life. It was clear to me then how bad we had all become. And that I was on my own. I realized that if I wanted things to change, I would have to make it happen. Almost immediately I started researching the history of the trade. I learned about the first resistance, generations ago, and heard of the rumors that survivors still lived in the jungle. I began to look for them. And I found them. They were good people."

Her eyes suddenly stung as she remembered the day she stumbled on the group of nomads. Raldo had been the first to believe in her good intentions, and he had never stopped looking out for her from then on, even though it eventually cost him his life.

She tried to shake off her melancholy. "It helped," she continued, feeling a powerful release in finally saying all of this out loud. "Knowing that I was fighting back against my father helped me to endure all the injustice I witnessed during those years. And knowing I was outsmarting him helped me to endure his scorn and cruelty toward me. But even so, I was afraid of him from the moment I saw him beat that girl until the moment he died. So afraid that I couldn't even lift a hand to save myself when he had a sword to my heart. If Jonan hadn't been there, he would have killed me."

"What?" said Giles, startled into speech. "I can imagine he was angry when he found out about your activities, but surely he wouldn't have killed you. He would have known we wouldn't let him get away with that."

She gave a humorless laugh. "Wouldn't you? You wouldn't have known anything about it. He didn't try to kill me because of my role in the resistance, although I'm sure that was an extra motivation. He had planned all along to kill me, then to make it look like the Kyonans did it, so that he could start his war. He thought Balenol would be able to easily overpower the young, inexperienced Kyonan king, and then we would have a permanent source of slaves. But he knew that King Siloam would not go to war without a compelling reason."

Scarlett raised her eyebrows at the horrified shock on the two faces turned to her. Apparently this part of the story had not filtered back to them. She should have written more comprehensively about what had happened. But it didn't matter now. She took a deep breath, bringing her thoughts back to the crisis at hand.

"I'm sorry for the pain I've caused you. I truly am. I never wanted to injure the family. I wanted so much to tell you the truth. And I hope you can forgive me. But even if you can't, even if you stay angry with me forever, it's no reason to punish Jonan. Put me in the dungeons if you want retribution. But there's no reason for him to be there."

"I didn't put him in there to punish you," said Giles quietly. "And it's not quite true that there's no reason for him to be there. He came to Balenol the first time expressly to aid the resistance, did he not?"

"No, you're wrong," said Scarlett quickly. "He didn't know anything about it when he came. His connection to the resistance was through me." She saw that Giles looked skeptical, and she held his gaze earnestly. "It's true. I saw him come to the defense of a slave in the courtyard, and I sent people to bring him into the resistance."

"Well, even so," said Giles, his expression grave, "he took part in it. He also killed your father, who was a prominent member of court, as well as the Overseer of Slaves."

"To stop him from killing me!" Scarlett protested.

"So you say," said Giles, hurrying on as she opened her mouth to interrupt, "and I don't doubt you. But most people would never believe that explanation. I told you, the people want blood."

"Well they can't have his," said Scarlett, her teeth clenched. "You promised we'd be safe, Giles. It's the only reason King Calinnae allowed us to come. If you won't do it for my sake, you should protect Jonan for the sake of the country. He's here as an official emissary of his king this time, and Cal will not take it lightly if anything happens to him."

"Cal?" repeated Giles, his eyebrows raised.

"I told you in my letter, Jonan and King Calinnae are childhood friends. They see each other as brothers just as much as you and I see each other as brother and sister. Unless you want war after all, you shouldn't let harm befall Jonan."

Giles frowned thoughtfully as he answered. "Of course I don't want war. But there are others who would think it was worth it. Whatever you might think, I don't want to see Jonan killed. But the people are riled up now, and if it's between him and you, of course I'm going to do everything I can to keep you safe."

"Giles," said Scarlett, her voice calm and quiet. "If you allow Jonan to be executed in my place, I will never forgive you. I will not hesitate to do whatever it takes to prevent that. And I'm capable of more than you think I am."

"I told you, I'm not the one who wants to see him killed." Giles sounded frustrated. "But while you're tethered to him, you each endanger the other even more. Besides, there are...your marriage in itself has made some people angry. You seem to forget how prominent a figure you've always been. I'll be honest—your decision to ally yourself with a Kyonan, and one known to have been part of the slave resistance—has made things difficult for the crown."

"If you're waiting for an apology," said Scarlett flatly, "it's not coming."

"My point is," Giles continued, as if she hadn't spoken, "some powerful people would like very much to see you free of this...entanglement."

"This what?" Scarlett's voice was dangerously quiet.

"If you and Jonan were not tied together," Giles pushed on stubbornly, "people might be more willing to turn a blind eye toward your actions."

"At the cost of Jonan's life," Scarlett snapped.

"Not necessarily," countered Giles. "When exactly were you married, Scar?"

"Last autumn, a year ago," said Scarlett, surprised by the unexpected question. "Why?"

"Yes, I know it was last autumn, but when exactly?" pressed Giles. "When will it be a year?"

"Why?" asked Scarlett again, narrowing her eyes suspiciously.

"Well, like I said," Giles began, sounding almost eager, "I've been looking for a way to help you out of this mess, and I think I've found something. It's an old law, but as far as I can tell, it's still valid. It says that if a member of the court marries a foreign citizen without consent of the sovereign, the sovereign can annul the marriage within twelve months."

CHAPTER FIVE

Scarlett felt her mouth drop open in a very unladylike expression as Giles spoke, and for a moment after he was done she could only stare blankly at him.

"Annul my marriage?" she said at last, her voice sounding strange. "Have you lost your mind? How could you possibly think I would ever agree to that?"

"Well, strictly speaking, you don't have to agree," said Giles, clearly nettled by her reaction. "I just have to convince Uncle Siloam that—"

"Giles," cut in Aunt Mariska, her tone admonishing. "We agreed that we wouldn't force her to do anything."

Scarlett turned astonished eyes on her aunt, making no effort to hide the sense of betrayal she felt. "You knew about this, Aunt Mariska?" she demanded. "You thought it was a good idea to annul my marriage?"

"I just thought it was a good idea for you to know you had the option, that's all," her aunt responded quickly. "I can imagine that after all that happened in Kyona, and after your... your secret became known, you might be afraid to return to Nohl. But we're your family, Scarlett. You'll always be welcome with us, and I wanted you to know that you do have a home to come back to, whatever you might have thought." She hesitated. "Whatever you might have been encouraged to think."

Scarlett had been searching the older woman's eyes as she listened, and at her aunt's last addition, she thought she understood. Before she could respond, however, Giles cut in.

"What Mother is trying to say is that you belong here with us, Scarlett."

She scowled at her cousin. "If you can keep my neck out from under the blade, you mean."

He opened his mouth to reply, but she forestalled him. "Never mind that." She turned back to Aunt Mariska. "Unless I'm mistaken, what you're really trying to say is that you think I married Jonan because I was afraid I had no other prospects— even that he persuaded me to think so—and that even now, deep down, I might want a way out."

She looked between them, her expression stern. "Let me make a few things very clear. Firstly and most importantly, I love Jonan. I married him for no other reason, and I'm happy as his wife. I don't wish to discuss that any further. Secondly, he never put any kind of pressure on me to do anything, certainly not to marry him. Believe me, I would know. I passed from childhood to adulthood in the company of a master manipulator, and though I'm not proud of it, the truth is I'm extremely skilled at manipulating people myself. So you can take my word for it when I say that Jonan doesn't have a manipulative bone in his body. And finally, I didn't have to marry Jonan to remain in Kyona. King Calinnae is a good man, and he would certainly have offered me sanctuary without any such stipulation. I had nothing to gain by marrying Jonan except the pleasure of his company."

"Well, that's certainly true," muttered Giles. She glared at him, but he met her look squarely. "What? You have to admit I have a point. If not for your treasonous activities, you could have married literally any unmarried nobleman in Balenol. And while we were all less than impressed when we realized that your father had spirited you away to Kyona in such a fashion, at least he was attempting to negotiate your marriage with their king. Instead you come back married to a commoner who, as far as I understand it, has no title, no land, and no fortune to speak of. And, if memory serves, quite a smart mouth on him."

Scarlett bristled instantly in Jonan's defense. "How dare you talk about him like that? What is it to you anyway? If you really cared about my well-being, you wouldn't be complaining that I didn't make an advantageous marriage. I'm a hundred times happier with him than I was living with one of the most powerful noblemen in Balenol. Yes, happier even than I was living here at the castle, surrounded by royalty."

"Does he really make you so happy, darling?" Aunt Mariska asked, a hint of longing in her voice. "Does he look after you? Is he kind to you?"

Scarlett turned to her aunt at once, softening. "Yes, Auntie, he really does. He is the best husband I could ask for. Our lives are simple because we choose it that way. We could live in the castle at Kynton if we wanted to, but we prefer to live in the forest. King Calinnae wanted to give Jonan an official title, but Jonan has no interest in such things. But it's not true that he has no position. We're the leaders of a substantial community of returned Kyonans and others who do not wish for city life. They all love Jonan. He leads them well, and he does so without expecting the acclaim or recognition of a title."

She could see that her words had put Aunt Mariska more at ease, but Giles wasn't so easily impressed.

"You are full of his praises," he said, his tone flat, "and you say that he would never put pressure on you. Does that mean that he didn't try to persuade you not to come back here?"

Scarlett matched him glare for glare. "He was only worried that I might be in danger. And it turns out he had good reason!"

Giles raised a skeptical eyebrow. "*Is* that all he was worried about? He wasn't also worried about giving your family the chance to remind you that you have options other than him?"

Remembering her conversation with Jonan on deck that morning, Scarlett had to admit to herself that Giles's words were uncomfortably close to the truth. She flushed and looked away, but not quickly enough to miss the sardonic curl of Giles's lip. He clearly knew that he had hit the mark.

"Evidently he had reason to be worried about that too," she said.

"And yet you defend him," growled Giles. "What kind of a man corners a woman into marrying him? He obviously knew you were much too good for him, and he didn't have a hope of succeeding if he pursued you honorably, so he—"

"It wasn't like that at all!" cried Scarlett, stung.

How was Giles managing to make the story of her marriage —which she had thought almost like something out of a fairy-tale—seem sordid and dishonorable? She took a deep breath.

"It doesn't matter what you think, Giles. I was of age before we married. The marriage was legal and binding, and there is no way I would consider trying to have it set aside."

"Not even to save his life?" Giles asked.

"What do you mean?" asked Scarlett uneasily.

"I've told you," said Giles, "there are powerful people who want your blood, as much for marrying Jonan as for your involvement in the resistance. People who are willing to do whatever it takes to remove the disgrace of your...alliance. I can't see any way to be sure of your safety except to separate you from him. If that...problem was taken care of, then I think we could convince my uncle the king to pass a lesser sentence than execution on Jonan. Not everyone would be satisfied, but that can't be helped. Some kind of justice could be seen to be done, and he could be allowed to return home to Kyona in one piece."

"With a few lashes, but without his wife," said Scarlett flatly. "Quite apart from everything else, do you think I'm going to stand by while he gets publicly flogged, or worse?"

Giles shrugged dismissively. "Jonan's tough, he can withstand whatever punishment might be applied. And," he reminded her, "you wouldn't be his wife if the king annuls the marriage."

Scarlett balled her fists at her side, but her voice was steady. "No thanks. I don't like that solution to my 'problem'."

"You don't have to like it," Giles snapped. "But I'm guessing you like the alternative even less." She raised her eyebrows inquiringly, and he pushed on. "Having the marriage set aside is not the only way to separate you and your husband. Or don't Kyonan marriage ceremonies include the phrase, 'until death do us part'?"

She sucked in a breath as she understood his meaning. "So you're telling me that Jonan will be executed unless I agree to this plan? That's outrageous. You're the one who assured me it was safe for us to come here. So you need to find a way out of this mess that doesn't involve anyone dying."

"I'm trying, Scarlett, I really am," he said, frustrated. "I don't want to force you to leave your husband any more than I want to see him executed. But I can't guarantee your safety any other way. You being executed yourself is still a very real possibility. And I'm not going to let that happen. But you just don't understand how bad things have been this last year. The crown is hanging onto its credibility by a thread. I thought I could contain things, but then *he* showed up, and started riling everyone up. Now they're all cursing the Kyonans with every second breath, and meanwhile in walks Jonan, the perfect target for all the pent-up rage...I don't see how the king can get out of this without doing *something* to Jonan at the very least."

Scarlett frowned, trying to keep up. "Who started riling everyone up? We both know that King Siloam isn't the one pulling any strings. Who's in his ear now?"

Giles exchanged a glance with his mother, and she was the one who answered, her voice soft.

"Your brother."

"Scanlon?" asked Scarlett, surprised, and Aunt Mariska nodded.

"He showed up in Nohl two weeks ago. Giles had written to inform him of your impending visit, as was only fair. We thought he might want to see you and meet your husband. He has barely shown his face since your father died. But now he's demanding justice for his murder. He and the men he brought with him—"

"He brought men?" Scarlett interrupted, beginning to feel uneasy, and her aunt nodded, her grave expression telling Scarlett that she was not the only one who sensed the threat behind Scanlon's actions.

"They've been spreading all kinds of discontent," Aunt Mariska continued. "Telling people that the Kyonans have effectively crippled us and that we should strike back. And he's had plenty to say about you, as well. The way he talks, you'd think Jonan had corrupted you, used you to destroy the slave system, then carried you forcibly back to Kyona as the spoils of war."

"What?" Scarlett demanded, startled. "That doesn't even make sense! The resistance was happening years before Jonan came, and the slaves didn't leave until well after he'd returned to Kyona."

"People don't care about the details," said Giles dryly. "Thanks to Scanlon, most of them now believe that Jonan was the one who started the resistance and that your involvement in it was entirely his doing, presumably as a result of him seducing you. They also believe that he took you with him by force when he returned to Kyona, and that your father followed you there only to be killed by Jonan while attempting to retrieve you."

Scarlett's mouth was hanging open in horror by the end of Giles's speech. For a moment she was at a loss for what to say in response to this disgustingly twisted version of the truth.

Giles took advantage of her stupefaction to add, "There wasn't time to write and stop you from coming. But the situation being what it now is, Jonan was in danger of falling afoul of an angry mob the moment he set foot in Nohl. The dungeons are honestly the safest place for him."

Scarlett shot him a look, but didn't think that this absurdity warranted further response. "What does Scanlon hope to gain by all this? I can't imagine he actually wants me back in Balenol. Does he just want to see Jonan and me both killed for revenge?"

Giles shrugged. "I was hoping you could tell me. You know him better than I do."

"Do I?" asked Scarlett doubtfully. "Honestly, I don't really know him at all. I was just a baby when I left father's estates to come and live at the castle. By the time I went to live with father at his manor house in Nohl, Scanlon was an adult, and whenever father was here, Scanlon stayed on the estates to take charge. We saw each other rarely, and our only interactions were superficial."

"Well, I suggest you have a less superficial conversation with him in the very near future if you want Jonan's head to stay on his shoulders," said Giles dryly. "Because unless I'm much mistaken, he's the one we'll need to convince that annulling your marriage and inflicting some non-fatal punishment on Jonan is enough. He's claiming to be the one who has been wronged, both by your father's death and by your marriage, and you have to admit that there's some truth to what he says."

"Why in the kingdom would I have to admit any such thing?" demanded Scarlett indignantly. "I fail to see what my marriage has to do with Scanlon. And as we've already established, there will be no annulment."

"Don't be difficult, Scar," said Giles wearily. "As your brother, and the head of your house now your father is dead, he would expect to have some say in your marriage. Or did Jonan undertake negotiations with him that I haven't heard about? Offered a generous settlement, perhaps?"

"No need to be sarcastic," snapped Scarlett. "It's not becoming for a prince."

"Children," said Aunt Mariska reprovingly, for all the world as if they were still ten years old, arriving for dinner late and covered in mud from sneaking off to play in the jungle.

"Mother is right," said Giles, his expression unyielding. "We need to take this situation seriously. How urgently do we need to act, Scarlett? When exactly will the first year of your marriage be over?"

Scarlett took a deep breath, for show, trying to seem as if she was considering whether to cooperate. "In two weeks," she lied smoothly. "Two weeks and two days, to be precise."

It wasn't difficult to lie convincingly. As sad as it was to admit to herself, deceit was second nature to Scarlett. It required much more effort to be honest. And as much as she had tried to improve in that area, she felt no qualms about her dishonesty in this situation. She needed to buy them some time.

Giles nodded thoughtfully, unsuspecting. "That's good. We have a little while to work out the details, figure out how to sell this solution."

Scarlett was silent, her expression giving nothing away. But inside her mind was whirring, already trying to formulate her own plan. She hoped that Jonan hadn't said anything to anyone about tomorrow being their anniversary. She couldn't imagine why he would have, but it still made her nervous to think of what Giles would do if he knew that this was his last day to put his "solution" into action. Especially since he apparently didn't need her to actually agree in order to make it happen. She had no doubt he could convince King Siloam to declare her marriage invalid. It was a well-known fact that the Balenan king was maddeningly—and dangerously—persuadable.

Giles's assertion that her options were to leave Jonan or see him executed was terrifying. She had to find a way out, and quickly. And Giles's idea wasn't even an option. Just that morning she had rebuked Jonan for even entertaining the thought that she would consider leaving him.

Besides, even if Giles could sell his best case scenario to the embittered populace, she knew his plan would never work. There was no way Jonan would leave Balenol without her, no matter how invalid the king might declare their marriage to be, and no matter how much his life was threatened. Even if they shipped him home in chains, he would just come back for her, probably at the head of Cal's army.

She restrained a groan. What a mess they were in. Jonan had been right—they should never have left Kyona.

"Well, there's nothing more we can do right now," Giles was saying. "You must be tired. A room has been prepared for you. I'll have someone show you—"

"What?" protested Scarlett. "I don't want to rest. I want to see Jonan, and talk to him. And we need to get him out of the dungeons immediately. I'll go down and—"

"Not possible," said Giles uncompromisingly.

"Giles—"

"I mean it, Scarlett," Giles said. "Jonan is in the dungeons to placate those who wanted to kill him the moment he arrived. We need it to seem that we are taking firm action, at least until we figure out how to win people over to a less bloodthirsty approach. If you wander in and out of there at will, it's not going to seem like his imprisonment is real. You know as well as I do that there are always watching eyes in the castle."

"So you expect me to go and relax while my husband rots in a cell?"

"Stop being melodramatic, Scarlett," said Giles in a long-suffering voice. "He'll be fine for one day. Tomorrow we'll—"

"Tomorrow?!" Scarlett cried, aghast. "It's not even noon yet. You want him to be in there all day and all night?"

Giles shrugged. "As I've explained multiple times, it's not me who wants him in there."

Scarlett opened her mouth to protest further, but stopped short at a sudden thought. As little as she wanted Jonan to be stuck in a prison cell for twenty-four hours, by tomorrow it would be too late to have their marriage annulled, even under Giles's obscure law. "Well, at least tell me you're going to send food this time."

She saw Giles's features ripple slightly at the reminder that this was not the first time Jonan had been thrown into these particular dungeons, but he didn't comment on it.

"Of course he will be fed," he said with dignity. "We are not barbarians."

CHAPTER SIX

Scarlett followed the servant summoned by Giles to her assigned room, but she didn't stay there for long. She was humming with nervous energy and had no desire to lie down. She had been less than impressed to discover she was expected to attend a banquet that evening.

Initially planning to defy Giles in the matter, she thought better of it when she discovered the king himself had invited her. She knew from her years living in the castle that to refuse an invitation from the sovereign would be a serious offense. It galled her to attend a feast while Jonan was locked away, but she didn't think it would help him if she put King Siloam off side.

In the hours before the meal, she wandered the halls of what had been her home for most of her life. The hardness she had cultivated in her role as rebel leader wasn't natural to her—in reality, she was a sentimental person. She berated herself for that sentiment now. She had imagined taking Jonan to the places of her childhood, showing him more of her world. Look where that desire had landed them.

Of course she thought about ignoring Giles's warning and going to the dungeons in search of Jonan, but she was not given the opportunity. From the moment she left her appointed room, she was followed by two royal guards, a fact that irritated her more than it surprised her. She had no doubt they would prevent her from entering the dungeons. It seemed she really would have to wait until the next day to speak with her husband.

Her aunt met her at her room to escort her down to the meal, a sign of solidarity that Scarlett appreciated, despite the uncertain expression on the older woman's face when she saw Scarlett's distinctly Kyonan dress.

"You didn't want to change, Scarlett?" she asked tentatively.

"No," said Scarlett stubbornly. "I didn't. I'm here as an official emissary of King Calinnae, and in that capacity I will attend the meal."

Her aunt made no further comment, but she wasn't the only one who noticed Scarlett's silent statement. Giles gave her a pointed look when she entered the banquet hall, and she saw a few raised eyebrows from some of the courtiers. Of course, the murmuring sweeping the room at her entrance could just as easily have been about her as about her dress.

Not that she cared. She was genuinely unconcerned about the opinion of these people. She'd never had much respect for most of them. It was uncomfortable, of course, to be so conspicuous. She felt a brief wish that Jonan could be by her side, but the thought was quickly banished. He would be even more conspicuous than she was, and much more likely to create animosity with his behavior.

King Siloam was seated in an ornate chair at the head of the long banquet table. As was customary, Scarlett and Aunt Mariska joined the stream of guests waiting in line to greet their royal host.

"Ah, Lady...Lady Wrendal," said the king vaguely as Scarlett rose from her curtsy. Scarlett refrained from rolling her eyes at the way he searched for her name, as if she had not grown up in his very castle.

"Your Majesty," she said politely. "Actually, I discarded that title upon my marriage."

"Your marriage? Ah yes, of course," said King Siloam, betraying a slight interest. "I remember now. Giles was speaking to me about you just this afternoon. It seems you have gotten yourself into some trouble, and need my assistance to extricate yourself from the entanglement."

He gave her what he evidently felt was a stern look, but his features were too habitually relaxed for it to be convincing. "You should take more care, my dear. You should not have allowed yourself to be tricked into taking part in some outlandish foreign ceremony. It seems that my nephew has been quite clever in finding a way out of your difficulties. I am sure you must be most grateful to him."

Scarlett's indignation grew throughout this speech. She kept her face blank only with great difficulty.

"There is some misunderstanding, Your Majesty," she began through gritted teeth. "It is not at my request that—"

"Yes, yes, Giles explained all the details," said King Siloam, waving a dismissive hand. "I am willing to help you, for your poor father's sake if nothing else. But later. Giles will arrange the practicalities, I'm sure."

Scarlett opened her mouth to protest further, but her aunt pulled her away. Already they had occupied the king's attention for an unusually long time, and a line of impatient courtiers had formed behind them.

Scarlett felt a flush of dual anger and embarrassment pass over her as she saw the interest of those behind them in the exchange. No doubt they would believe she regretted her marriage and her alliance with Kyona and had begged Giles to help her get out of it. Well, it served her right for thinking she didn't care what these people thought.

Of more pressing concern was the fact that Giles had acted so quickly. Perhaps she shouldn't have pretended to go along with him. She could only be thankful that the king was not exactly one to show initiative. She felt cold all over as she imagined how easily a more engaged sovereign could have expeditiously dealt with the matter that very afternoon.

As she turned away from the king, her eyes fell on a small knot of people on the other side of the banquet hall. She recognized the general of the king's army, and a couple of lords who often hung around him. Her father used to be one of those lords, she realized with a strange pang. She couldn't quite find it in herself to regret his death, but the construction that, according to Giles, was being placed on the event made her feel dirty whenever she thought about it.

She was still watching the general when he shifted to the side, allowing her a glimpse of the man with whom he was talking. She froze at the sight of the young man's undeniably handsome, and familiar, features. It seemed that Scanlon had taken his father's place in that faction of the court. Not that he looked anything like their father. On the contrary, he was almost a male version of Scarlett, except for his eyes. They were darker than hers, and their calculating gleam suggested a physical resemblance to the former Lord Wrendal that wasn't really there.

Scarlett's eyes narrowed as she noted the confident manner in which her brother was speaking with these much older, much more senior noblemen. She started across the room before she fully knew what she was doing. In the back of her mind she knew that a public confrontation wasn't wise. But it had been a very trying day, and here, it seemed, was the source of all her problems.

"Lady Wrendal! You are back among us! And, I need hardly add, as radiant as ever."

Scarlett turned with a sigh. It seemed she would be rescued from her rash intentions after all. The man who was addressing her had been one of her most determined suitors before her sudden departure from Balenol.

"It's not Lady Wrendal anymore, My Lord," she said as patiently as she could manage. "I am married now."

The man instantly looked somber, but although he lowered his voice, he spoke just as eagerly. "Indeed, My Lady, I am aware of what has occurred. I was shocked—most shocked—to hear of how you were imposed upon. I can only be glad that the scoundrel has been thrown into the dungeons. I know that some have made unjust accusations, but I want you to know that I have never wavered in my devotion. I am confident that no blame attaches to you and, indeed, I am as eager as ever to do whatever might please you. I only wish I could have had the honor of championing you amidst all those Kyonan barbarians. But now, at least, we have you safely back among us."

Scarlett heard all of this with an impassive face. When he had finished, she closed her eyes, willing herself to keep her temper.

"I am sorry to bring it up," the nobleman blundered on hastily, misinterpreting her reaction. "Of course the topic would distress you. Let us think of more pleasant things. May I escort you for the duration of the banquet?"

Scarlett allowed herself one brief moment of fantasizing about how easy it would be to silence this man's impertinent tongue. She never went anywhere unarmed, after all, and she could feel the steel of her dagger against her leg, where it was concealed. It would take only seconds to whip it out, and only seconds more to—but she exercised her considerable self-control to cut off those thoughts. Hadn't she just been telling Giles that she took no pleasure in any of the violence?

"I am honored, but I must decline your escort," she said instead, her tone polite but not friendly. "As I said, I am a married woman, and I don't think my husband would appreciate the offer. His current situation is the result of a mistake and is, I assure you, temporary."

Infuriatingly, instead of accepting the rebuff, the man just lowered his voice even further. "Your discretion is to be applauded, My Lady. But truly, you have no need to fear him now. He is incarcerated—I overheard a group of soldiers discussing it as they came out of the dungeons just a couple of hours ago—and you are safely among your own people now."

Scarlett's patience was beginning to wear thin. "Stop calling me My Lady. And I am not afraid of my—wait." She paused as she caught up with the rest of what the nobleman had said. "Why was a group of soldiers coming from the dungeons only a couple of hours ago? They took Jonan there early this morning."

"Perhaps they were changing shifts," said the nobleman dismissively, but Scarlett frowned.

"Not if they were soldiers. The dungeons are the province of the royal guard."

"Indeed," said her admirer lightly. "Thankfully not the province of lovely ladies such as yourself. Let us speak of other matters." He looked around at the sudden bustle of movement. "Ah, I see we are being summoned for the meal to begin."

Scarlett saw that he was right, and she followed him mechanically toward the king's enormously long, heavily laden banquet table. She was lost in her thoughts, feeling a nebulous alarm about her companion's revelations, and she was seated before she realized that she had allowed the nobleman to escort her after all. She restrained a groan. She had intended to find her aunt when it was time to be seated, in the hope that she could be placed next to one of her three male cousins.

Once everyone was seated, the guests all fell silent, looking respectfully toward the king at the head of the table. He acknowledged their attention with a regal nod, then gestured toward his brother in a mute invitation for him to conduct the formal welcome.

Prince Rupert stood, and Scarlett noted that her uncle looked visibly older than he had a year ago. Evidently the stress of the country's condition was taking its toll. She felt a twinge of guilt and firmly suppressed it. A familiar process.

Uncle Rupert hadn't sought her out to greet her since her arrival that morning, a fact that she had found noteworthy but not surprising. She respected her uncle much more than King Siloam, and she was glad that he was the king's heir, and Giles his heir. But there was no love between them exactly. Although he had never given her reason to think he begrudged giving her houseroom after her mother died, he had not accepted her as a daughter the way his wife had.

"I am honored," he began in his clear, confident voice, "to welcome you on my brother the king's behalf. It is the crown's delight to have you all present at the king's banquet table. As you are all no doubt aware, the purpose of this banquet is in part to mark the return to Balenol of my niece, Lady Scarlett Wrendal—" his eyes flicked to Scarlett and took in the challenge in her eyes, "—as she has been known to us."

The amendment didn't entirely satisfy Scarlett, but it was something. As soon as her uncle had looked away, she had schooled her face back to an expressionless mask, as was habitual. She was sure no one would guess her surprise, but the truth was she had not expected a formal mention in the welcome speech.

As Uncle Rupert continued talking, many pairs of eyes were

fixed on her. Some faces showed only the admiration she had become used to since reaching womanhood, but more of the guests were looking at her with steely, even angry expressions.

"I know that given her recent sojourn in Kyona, Lady Wrendal's presence here is a reminder to us all that we have not yet achieved full resolution of the Kyonan issue that has affected us this last year. However, I trust that you will join me in regarding this long-awaited return as a sign that the crown is committed to finding a solution that is satisfactory to all. I for one will be most interested to hear a full account of the trade treaty being considered between our king," he nodded toward his brother, "and the Kyonan crown."

He raised his glass and held it toward Scarlett in a gesture that was almost, but not quite, a toast in her honor.

Scarlett restrained a sigh, and not just because the supposed treaty was mainly a fabrication on Giles's part to justify her presence in Nohl. Cal wasn't necessarily closed to the idea in future, but opening diplomatic relations with the kingdom that had exploited their people for generations wasn't a high priority for the young king.

Uncle Rupert most likely knew all this—he certainly hadn't promised a commitment on either side. He was very good at being diplomatic. At *almost* saying a great many things without actually committing to anything.

"May we successfully balance justice for the past and progress toward the future," he was continuing. "To Balenol."

"To Balenol," was repeated around the table as everyone joined the toast and drank deeply. Many pairs of eyes were still on Scarlett, some simply curious, others openly hostile. Feeling cornered, and not wanting to make a statement at that moment, she also drank to the toast.

A burning passed through her as Uncle Rupert sat down. His speech had been exactly what she might have expected.

Acknowledging the controversy of her presence without giving anything to anyone. No mention of Jonan—it was as if her husband didn't exist, as if she had merely gone for a holiday to Kyona and was now back to stay. She wanted to hurl her goblet against the wall, but she was fully aware of how many people were still watching her.

So instead she sat silently, her expression serene. She felt a sudden, potent longing for her new home in the Kyonan forest community. She had almost forgotten how it felt to be constantly watched, unalterably conspicuous. She was out of practice, and it made the unrelenting vigilance all the more exhausting. She had thought she was done with all this forever. If only she could be with Jonan instead of surrounded by these artificial smiles, all hiding either shallow folly or selfish scheming. She would genuinely rather be spending the evening in the dungeons with her husband.

But that option had not been given to her. So instead she had to endure the prattle of her self-appointed escort throughout the meal. His avowals of constancy, and his apparent determination to stand by her despite the ire of those who wanted her executed, would be touching if she wasn't fully aware that his devotion was entirely driven by her beauty.

She remembered again Jonan declaring when they met that he was not so easily impressed as to admire her for her beauty, and she suddenly yearned for her husband so intensely that it felt like physical hunger. The unspoken fondness in one of his smiles was worth more than a hundred of this nobleman's superficial compliments.

The most irritating thing about the evening was how pleased Giles looked every time he looked over to see her sitting, apparently contentedly, beside her former suitor. His face seemed to say, "See, you still have excellent prospects here". She would have liked to wither Giles with a glare, but with so many others watching her, she held her peace.

She couldn't get out of sitting next to the nobleman at the meal, but she could, and did, refuse to dance with him once the music struck up. She was polite but unyielding in her refusal, and he wasn't the only young hopeful disappointed at her insistence that her status as a married woman precluded her from dancing.

She wasn't surprised to hear the whole range of reactions as people muttered about her and the supposed trade arrangement. Before arriving in Balenol, she would have expected almost everyone to spurn the idea of trading with the kingdom they so despised. But having seen for herself the poverty brought about by the slaves' departure, she could understand why some thought it worth considering.

What did surprise her, however, were the murmurs she heard about dragons. When last she had been in Nohl, no one in the city believed in the creatures of legend, herself included. She knew that word would have spread of the dramatic appearance of the dragon Elddreki during the confrontation between the Kyonan king and the Balenan delegation, assisted by Kyonan allies who were enemies to Cal. But still, it had never occurred to her to think that anyone might connect her visit with the magic beasts.

No one asked her outright, but she formed the distinct impression from various veiled comments and questions, that a trade treaty might not be the only benefit some were expecting from her arrival. It seemed that rumors had spread that she might have returned with the intention of making amends to her homeland by offering Balenol some unspecified connection to the creatures' power.

Unease curled through her stomach. An exaggerated trade treaty was one thing, but she didn't think any good could come from creating vast expectations that she would never be able to fulfill.

Shaking off her admirers, she wended her way around the room, looking for her brother. He was once again speaking with the general, but this time the two of them were alone. Seeing how earnestly they were conversing, she checked her rising desire to confront Scanlon, and changed course. Edging around the room, she placed herself to one side of a large suit of armor, just close enough to hear what they were saying if she strained her ears.

"The young prince had him thrown straight into the dungeons, my men tell me," the general was saying. "I'm not sure how that serves our purposes. Unless you've changed your mind, and want the crown to execute him after all."

"Of course not," said Scanlon lazily. "I don't often change my mind. But the crown won't execute him. My cousin is busily looking for a peaceful way out—haven't you heard the rumors? Things are proceeding as smoothly as we could wish. The crown will spare my sister's precious mongrel, rest assured."

Scarlett frowned, and not because of Scanlon's insulting way of speaking about Jonan. The fact that her brother apparently didn't want her husband to be executed should have been a relief, but it somehow sounded sinister instead.

"My Lady." For a moment Scarlett thought one of her admirers had followed her, but the sneering tone of the salutation suggested otherwise. "You are quite...courageous to return here after word of your activities spread. One can only assume that life in Kyona was not all you hoped it would be."

Scarlett glared at the speaker, an obnoxious and particularly oily member of court. His rudeness didn't trouble her, but his raised voice did.

"On the contrary, Lord Grentan," she said bitingly. "I returned merely to visit my family. You would be astonished at the refinement of Kyonan society. It makes our ways look barbaric by comparison."

"I confess, My Lady," said Lord Grentan coldly, "such a discovery would astonish me."

If only the man would lower his voice. But a quick glance showed Scarlett that it was too late anyway. Scanlon and the general had become aware of her conversation, and both men were now steadily regarding her.

"It is no longer My Lady," she snapped at the nobleman in front of her. "And if you'll excuse me, my family reunion is not quite complete."

She turned away without waiting for a response and strode boldly up to Scanlon and his companion.

"Scanlon." Her voice was as cold as ice. "It has been a long time."

"Welcome, sister," Scanlon said, the slight sneer that accompanied his half-bow so comfortable on his face that she doubted he had done it consciously. The expression was so reminiscent of their father that it threw Scarlett off balance for a moment.

"I haven't felt much by way of welcome, Scanlon," she said. "My husband is in a cell, and I'm being watched like a criminal myself."

Scanlon raised his eyebrows. "None of that is my doing," he said lightly. "Surely your Kyonan was arrested under orders of the crown. And you must admit there's reason. He's guilty of conspiring against the crown, isn't he? Did he not escape from the very same dungeons the last time he was here?"

Scarlett snorted. The general looked startled at the unladylike sound, but Scarlett was far beyond caring.

"He was imprisoned because of me, not because of any action he took against the crown. I'm flattered that you rate my importance so high, Scanlon, but I'm not royalty. The crime for which he was arrested last time, as I suspect you are well aware, was kissing me in our father's presence. And no conspiracy was required—I was perfectly willing."

A shadow passed briefly over Scanlon's smooth features before he was able to contain it. Scarlett was pleased to have goaded him into giving himself away even in this small way. Clearly her role in the resistance was not the chief issue for Scanlon. Her romantic entanglement with a Kyonan offended and enraged him, just as it had their father.

"But don't worry," she said casually. "He more than atoned for the impertinence by marrying me."

Scanlon ground his teeth slightly, and Scarlett allowed herself a small smirk. Yes, he was definitely outraged by her choice of husband.

"Now he can kiss me every day," she continued blithely. "And just imagine how beautiful our children will be. Don't you think the blend of Balenan and Kyonan features will produce gorgeous offspring?"

She could see that Scanlon was close to the edge, and she couldn't resist continuing. She wasn't really sure what she hoped to gain by baiting him, but it was certainly satisfying to watch the vein throb in his temple.

"I hope you'll come to Kyona to visit us, Scanlon. You'll want to meet your nieces and nephews, of course."

"Your vulgarity in speaking of such things is offensive," Scanlon hissed, his restraint finally cracking. "And I refuse to own relationship with any Kyonan brats." He paused, taking a deep breath. "Not that it matters, because you will not be returning there, Scarlett. I am the head of our house now, and you will do as I tell you."

"You may be the head of the house of Wrendal," said Scarlett, raising an eyebrow, "but I no longer belong to that house." Scanlon's jaw twitched, and suddenly Scarlett dropped the act.

"What do you want, Scanlon?" she asked seriously. "I know

you've been spreading lies about Jonan and me, stirring people up. And don't try to convince me that you're motivated by grief for our dear father. I may not know you very well, but I know you well enough not to believe that. What do you hope to gain by all this? Is it just about revenge? Because if you want to punish me, do so. Leave Jonan out of it."

"You wish to shield your mongrel husband, do you?" sneered Scanlon. "How noble."

"Noble?" Scarlett retorted. "Not at all. I'm just a commoner now. Like our mother."

She saw another flicker in Scanlon's eyes and knew that she had once again hit home. So their mother's common blood was a source of shame to him, was it? How like their father he was. Which meant that, whatever he was doing, he was playing a deep game.

"You wrong me," he said at last, ignoring her comment. "I am not so petty as to seek revenge. I wish only to do my duty. Now that I am the head of the house, it falls to me to protect my foolish, vulnerable sister from the schemes of the Kyonans, whom we all know to be inherently untrustworthy. Besides, as I already said, it was not I who gave the order to have your Kyonan arrested. Speak to our cousin if you wish to rescue him from the dungeons."

Scarlett was silent for a long moment, looking her brother up and down. "I don't know what your game is, Scanlon," she said at last. "But I know who is and isn't trustworthy without any help from you. Yes, I was angry that Giles had Jonan imprisoned. But at least I know he did it out of a genuine desire to protect me. Misguided, but genuine. You, on the other hand, only intend harm."

Without giving him a chance to reply, she turned and walked deliberately away from them. Her keen ears picked up her brother's voice, low and furious, as he addressed the general who had listened in silent astonishment to the whole interchange.

"You see why it is necessary to act. You will have your opening, I promise you."

Scarlett didn't break stride, walking determinedly all the way out of the banquet hall, ignoring anyone who tried to hail her. She frowned over Scanlon's words all the way up to her room. She wasn't sure what exactly he was up to, but she had a feeling that she needed to stop him, for the sake of more lives than just Jonan's.

CHAPTER SEVEN

Before she even opened her eyes, Scarlett was aware of a nagging sense of incompleteness. Something was missing. Instinctively, she reached out a hand. It met empty sheets, and she suddenly remembered.

She prolonged opening her eyes for a moment longer, wishing all her problems would go away if she just refused to look at them. How could she already feel so exhausted before even rising from her night's rest? Not that it had been a very restful night. It was the first since her wedding that she had spent alone, and she had slept only fitfully, unable to help picturing Jonan stretched out uncomfortably in the dungeon.

Today was their anniversary. While she was glad to welcome the day that had, by simply dawning, removed one of the dangers facing her, it was not exactly how she had expected to spend her first anniversary. For one thing, she had anticipated waking with her husband beside her.

It didn't seem like so much to ask.

Opening her eyes at last, she noted with surprise that it was still dim. Dawn had only just broken. She wondered why she had woken so early—she felt as though she had been pulled from a deep sleep. The thought no sooner passed through her mind than she registered a knocking at the door, and realized that she had been woken by the sound.

"Scarlett!" The muffled voice made her spring upright. Even through the solid wooden door, she recognized it. "Scarlett, come quickly! Something's happening in the courtyard."

"Coming, Aunt Mariska!"

She grabbed the closest dress to hand, a green one that was laid across a chair, and threw it on at random before hurrying to open the door.

"There you are!" her aunt cried. "Why was the door locked?"

Scarlett shrugged. "You can't be too careful. What's happening?"

Aunt Mariska gave her a strange look as she began to lead Scarlett down the corridor, but didn't comment further. "It's Jonan. They're bringing him up from the dungeons."

"At this hour?" Scarlett asked, confused. "I know Giles said he was going to look into releasing him today, but why so early?"

"It wasn't Giles," said Aunt Mariska grimly. "He didn't give the order. He's gone to try to sort it out now, but I thought I'd do best to let you know what's happening. I thought you'd want to know immediately, not after it's all over."

"Thank you," said Scarlett, reaching out and squeezing her aunt's hand as they hurried along. "You were right."

It wasn't until they were crossing the castle's wide entryway that Scarlett realized why she felt strange. The dress she had thrown on was not one that she had brought with her from Kyona. On the contrary, it was distinctly Balenan. It was cut in the style that she had worn up until her departure from Nohl but that would be considered outrageous in Kyona, leaving her arms and shoulders completely bare. She scowled. One of the servants must have laid it out for her. She wondered who was responsible for this officious interference.

All thoughts of her attire fled at the sight that met her eyes as they emerged into the courtyard in front of the castle. She supposed the scene should not have come as a surprise after Aunt Mariska had told her that the commotion was in the courtyard rather than the castle, but Scarlett was still unprepared for the sight of her husband at the whipping post. In her first sweeping glance she took in the group of soldiers surrounding him, instantly recognizing the apparent leader. He had been her father's favorite lackey, and he was particularly bloodthirsty.

But as soon as Scarlett's eyes fell on Jonan, she had no attention for anyone else. He was shirtless, presumably having been stripped in preparation for the intended whipping, and she could see lacerations and bruises all over his chest.

"Jonan!" she cried involuntarily, starting forward in horror.

He turned his head quickly at her voice, and she felt as though her heart stopped as she took in the bruise blooming under one eye and the matted blood in his hair. Their eyes locked, his expression uncharacteristically hard to read, and she felt fury rising within her. How dare they beat him?

"The dungeons were the safest place for him, were they?" she spat at Giles, who was standing nearby. Other than shooting her a frown, he didn't respond. He was busy arguing with the head soldier. Predictably, Giles looked irritated but not nearly as worked up as the situation warranted.

Scarlett didn't stay to hear their argument, sweeping by her cousin as she rushed toward Jonan. But Giles was apparently paying more attention to her than she was to him, because he flung out an arm as she passed, pulling her to a halt.

"Let me go," she hissed, but Giles shook his head.

"Hold on, Scarlett," he said sternly. "Don't make the situation worse."

"Look at him, Giles!" she cried. "They've thrashed him, and they're about to flog him. How much worse can I make it?"

"You know exactly how much worse," he said shortly. "So stay out of this and let me handle it."

"Because you've done such a great job so far!" she cried, her voice sounding slightly hysterical even to her own ears. "Now let me go!"

"No," said Giles firmly, tightening his grip on her arm. A movement caught her attention, and she turned quickly back toward Jonan. He was still several yards away, but it was clear that he could hear their conversation. She had been surprised that he had been standing passively so far, but at Giles's refusal to let go of her arm, he began to struggle against his captors, his eyes narrowed in a glare directed at her cousin. One of the soldiers cuffed him around the head in response, and Scarlett broke free of Giles with a cry to race toward him.

Once again, she was restrained, this time by one of the soldiers standing immediately in front of Jonan. Her fingers itched to pull out her dagger, but Jonan's voice reminded her that it was up to her to stop this situation from exploding.

"Don't you *dare* lay a finger on her! Get your filthy hands off her right now!"

The soldier just snorted. "Not in a position to be making demands, are you, mongrel?"

"How dare you talk to him like that?!" Scarlett cried, even as the calculating part of her mind took note of the soldier's use of the insult, the same one Scanlon had applied to Jonan the night before. "And let me go at once! I want to speak to my husband!"

"You can speak to him from right here," said the soldier rudely. "And from what I hear, he won't be your husband for much longer." The man leaned forward, leering into her face, and Scarlett instinctively pulled back in disgust. "One way or the other."

The look on Jonan's face was as belligerent as ever, but Scarlett was alarmed to detect no surprise or confusion at the man's words. What had they been telling him? She gave up trying to break free of the soldier, and leaned around him.

"Jonan," she said, catching her husband's eye, but then faltered. She had been going to ask if he was all right, but it was a stupid question. He was clearly far from all right.

"Good to see you, Scarlett," he said, his voice deceptively casual. He gestured around them as well as he could with his bound hands. "Do you realize that this is the spot where we met? It's quite romantic, isn't it? Them bringing us here on our anniversary."

"Jonan," she choked out, hardly able to bear the sarcasm in his voice.

"Anniversary?" Giles had approached while she was distracted, and his words cut off whatever response she might have made. "You lied to me?"

She met his accusatory look coolly. "I did."

He made a noise of frustration. "Why? I could have sorted everything out yesterday if I'd known! Now how do you expect me to keep him alive?"

"I expect you to find a way," she snapped, turning back to Jonan. "What happened, Jo?" she asked urgently. "What did they do? Giles," she glared at her cousin, "assured me you would be safe, and fed, and—"

"Oh, the hospitality was first rate," said Jonan, still speaking in that horrible, sarcastic tone. "The best stale bread and hard cheese I've ever had." He looked her over quickly, and she didn't miss the way his eyes lingered on her bare shoulders. "Nothing to the king's banquet, from what I hear, but no matter. You know I was never that fond of Balenan food—or company—anyway."

Her heart wrenched as she detected the anguish lurking behind his words, his false tone suddenly making perfect sense to her. Clearly a beating was not all he had endured. Unlike her, Jonan was rarely hard to read, and she had no difficulty interpreting the vulnerability behind his bravado. The soldiers had been taunting him, she was certain.

Her eyes stung as she imagined what they might have said. Jonan had probably been expecting her to storm into the dungeons hard on his heels yesterday, demanding his release. Instead, he had heard nothing from her all day and all night, and had been treated to whatever warped description of her conduct his tormentors had seen fit to communicate.

How she had attended the king's banquet, at which no mention had been made of her imprisoned Kyonan husband. How she had spoken with the king on her entrance about finding a way to extricate her from her entanglement—how rumors had swirled that the king was going to annul her marriage. How she had been escorted throughout the banquet by one of her noble Balenan suitors. And now she appeared, dressed once again in the style of her homeland.

"Jonan," she whispered, willing him to ignore all the men around them, and listen only to her. "Have faith in me."

Her eyes bored into his as she reminded him subtly of their conversation back on the ship. His expression softened, his shoulders slumping slightly as he exhaled, releasing some of the tension he had been holding.

"Are you all right, Scarlett?" he asked softly, the bravado gone and his pain and weariness suddenly obvious. She wondered if he had slept at all. "They haven't hurt you, have they?"

"No, I'm not all right," she said, sudden tears springing into her eyes at his concern. "I've been here for one day, and my husband has been imprisoned, beaten and starved."

"Hardly starved," said Jonan with a smile. "I'm really fine, Scar, don't worry about me. At least they didn't put me in the execution chamber this time, so that's something."

"This is not what I call fine," said Scarlett, reaching a hand toward the bruise on Jo's face. But the soldier who was still gripping her arm pulled her back, not allowing her to reach Jonan.

"No fraternizing with the prisoner," the soldier barked.

Scarlett bristled, but before she could respond, the soldier in charge stepped forward to back his henchman up. Glaring at him, she realized that he was now holding the long and lethal whip that was once used regularly to discipline recalcitrant slaves.

"As he says, Lady Wrendal," the soldier smirked. "You should really move back. This whip has been known to ricochet back when *spectators...*" his gaze lingered unpleasantly on Jonan, focusing on the scar on his cheek, "...get too close."

Jonan growled at the implied threat to Scarlett, but that was the least of her concerns.

"You will not be lashing him," she snarled, her voice shaking with fury.

"My orders say otherwise," he responded insolently, his eyes roving lazily over her.

"Nonsense," said Giles briskly. "As I have already made clear, your orders are to return him to the dungeons."

"I think you mean release him," contradicted Scarlett, glaring at her cousin.

"I wasn't talking about your orders, *Your Highness*," the soldier drawled at Giles, before turning to Scarlett. "And certainly not yours."

"Whose, then?" demanded Giles, irate. "On whose orders did you remove this man from his cell, and under whose authority do you defy my direct instructions?"

"My general, of course," said the soldier, his air of innocence unconvincing. "Like any soldier, I follow my chain of command."

Giles narrowed his eyes. "You know the chain of command as well as I do, which means you are perfectly well aware that the general is outranked by the crown, including anyone in the direct line of succession."

The soldier didn't respond, just looked at Giles with an insolent expression that filled Scarlett with foreboding. She wasn't convinced that the general had actually ordered the violence against Jonan—she knew that this particular soldier had a grudge of his own against her husband—but it didn't matter. The open defiance of the hierarchy that placed the general under the crown was what alarmed her.

Glancing at Giles, she saw that the significance of the soldier's response was not lost on him, either. He frowned, but the expression was as indicative of thoughtfulness as anger. He would be interested in getting to the root of the matter, not in making a show of strength to this unimportant individual soldier. As the soldier turned back to Jonan, the whip still gripped in his hand, Scarlett realized that Giles was still deep in thought, deciding how best to respond to the bigger issue. He clearly didn't consider preventing Jonan from being flogged to be sufficiently important to justify playing his hand.

She, however, had quite a different opinion on the matter.

Another soldier was still loosely holding her arm, but she took him by surprise with the speed of her movement as she leaped forward, grabbing the head soldier's arm.

"Stop," she said, her voice infused with an authority she knew she didn't really possess. "You will not lash him."

"Won't I?" The soldier laughed unpleasantly. "I suggest you don't try to intervene in the criminal's punishment, My Lady," he said. "Or you might find yourself in difficulties of your own."

He spoke with such a sneer that Scarlett was left in no doubt as to the insincerity of his polite words. She glared at him, still gripping his arm, refusing to back down. The soldier noted her unyielding expression with amusement, his eyes lingering on her in a way she didn't like.

"Allow me to escort you to a safe distance," he said.

He twisted his arm with a swift motion at odds with his lazy words. Her grip on his arm was broken, and instead she found both of the soldier's hands spread across her shoulders as he pushed her backward, away from Jonan.

He grinned unpleasantly at her as he did so, and she caught her breath, as much at his lecherous expression as at the way his fingers splayed on her bare skin in a manner that felt intimate and intrusive. Her heart pounded uncomfortably as she felt his thumbs roaming over her collarbone, his hands stretched over an unnecessarily large area as he compelled her to move.

She had often been uncomfortable at the way this soldier had looked at her, but when she lived in her father's house he would never have dared to touch her. She had the distasteful impression that he was relishing an excuse to do so, and she had to admit that the action frightened her. It wasn't that she was worried he would overpower her, rather that it was fresh evidence of how little he recognized Giles's authority. He obviously had no fear of the displeasure of either her cousin or her husband, to leer at her in such a way with both of them present.

But one at least of those men he had underestimated.

"GET YOUR HANDS OFF HER!"

The soldier turned his head, and Scarlett felt a rush of mingled relief and alarm at Jonan's inevitable reaction to the soldier's manhandling. With a roar, Jonan broke free of the two soldiers holding him, starting toward the man whose hands still gripped Scarlett's shoulders. Several other soldiers leaped forward to restrain him, struggling to hold him in check.

The head soldier had tucked the whip under his arm when he had grabbed Scarlett, but he pulled it up now, letting go of her at last.

"Take him to the post," he spat, his expression ugly. "I

promised this mongrel a lashing a long time ago, and it's time I kept my word."

"You won't!" Scarlett cried, pulling out her dagger without further hesitation. She was done being diplomatic. At this moment she didn't care about the bigger picture, about Giles's solutions or Scanlon's plots. She was simply not going to allow her husband to be flogged like a criminal if she could possibly prevent it.

The soldier ignored her words, issuing a curt order over his shoulder. "Take her out of reach. Her time will come." He didn't even turn to look at her as he spoke, his eyes still trained maliciously on Jonan.

So much the better.

Making use of the advantage of surprise, Scarlett ducked low as a soldier approached her, slashing her blade across the man's knees. His cry of shock and pain had not yet penetrated to his leader's consciousness when Scarlett fell upon the head soldier, plunging her dagger into the arm that held the whip.

He gave an involuntary shout, dropping the weapon and clutching at the wound on his upper arm, from which blood was flowing freely. Scarlett darted around him, running purposefully toward the soldiers clustered around Jonan. They fell back a step in astonishment, and Scarlett reached her husband in seconds. Their eyes locked for an instant, and she smirked slightly at the appreciation in his eyes as he watched her performance. It was almost too easy. She could hear Giles shouting behind her, but she ignored him, turning her blade toward the ropes binding Jonan's hands.

"Seize her!" roared the head soldier.

But it was too late. Jonan was already free, and he lost no time in leaping in front of Scarlett, sweeping her behind him with one arm, heedless of the fact that he had no weapon.

Warmth rushed through her at the contact. Surely it hadn't been just one day since he had touched her. It felt like a week.

The soldier pulled out his sword in a swift motion, his face contorted with fury. Jonan squared his shoulders, his stance indicating that he was ready to fight, although with what Scarlett couldn't imagine. She was so focused on the duo that she didn't notice the soldier approaching immediately to her right, and she let out a startled cry as he grabbed her in belated obedience to his leader's order.

Jonan's attention instantly shifted to her, and before the soldier knew what he was about, he had landed a swift punch to the man's head. Scarlett's attacker dropped, senseless, to the ground.

Scarlett looked up from the man's form a moment before Jonan did, locking eyes with the head soldier. She sucked in a breath as she read the murderous intent in his eyes. Alerted by her expression, Jonan didn't even look behind him, just bent down to retrieve the sword of the unconscious soldier. In one swift motion he spun, the sword in front of him, in time to intercept the attack.

Scarlett saw Jonan's rage in the sudden stiffening of his frame as he grasped that the soldier's target was not him, but Scarlett. With deadly determination, Jonan lunged forward, interposing himself between his wife and the soldier bearing down on her. Scarlett barely had time to feel alarm before it was over. Experienced as he was, the soldier was no match for Jonan's hidden source of strength. With a swift clash of metal, her husband's sword forced its counterpart to the side and felled its wielder. Permanently.

The sudden stillness in the courtyard lasted only a moment before furious shouts rent the air. The remaining soldiers converged on Jo and Scarlett, and for a moment she thought they would both be killed on the spot.

"STOP!" Giles's authoritative voice rang across the courtyard, causing another momentary pause. He strode forward, his face furious.

"But Your Highness," protested one of the soldiers. "He just killed—"

"I am well aware of what happened," Giles snapped. "But my uncle's royal courtyard is no place for an angry mob. Restrain him, but no more bloodshed!"

"Giles!" protested Scarlett, as the soldiers sprang forward eagerly to seize Jonan, who looked mutinous but didn't actually resist.

Giles stared her down, unrepentant. "Don't start, Scarlett. You've already made enough of a mess."

Glancing around, she saw that the scene was indeed a mess, with the injured soldier on the ground, someone bending over him to look at his slashed knees, blood pooling around the dead soldier, and a substantial crowd beginning to gather around the edges of the courtyard.

"What were you thinking?" Giles admonished her, his face still furious as he grabbed her by the arm. "Your actions were outrageous. And you!"

His gaze swept over Jonan, now firmly held by two soldiers, only showing by the occasional shove of his elbow or shoulder that he was still defiant.

"Do you realize how hard I've been trying to keep you alive? You're doing everything you can to make that impossible for me. Both of you!" He glowered once again at Scarlett. "Your little stunt with the anniversary—"

"What are you talking about?" demanded Jonan. "What's our anniversary to you?"

Giles just glared at him, breathing hard, so Scarlett answered instead.

"Giles found some archaic law that would allow King Siloam to annul our marriage as long as he did it within the first year. To buy us time, I told him that our anniversary wasn't for a couple of weeks."

"Good thinking, Scar," said Jonan, but the savage approval in his voice gave her no satisfaction as he turned his gaze on Giles, an ugly look on his face. "I might have known you were behind this annulment rumor. I knew you would try to break us up the minute we set foot here."

"And *I* might have known that I have you to thank for encouraging my cousin's shameless dishonesty."

"How dare you criticize her—" Jonan started, but Scarlett cut him off.

"Don't be ridiculous, Giles," she snapped. "I've been deceiving you very successfully since long before I ever set eyes on Jonan. Now stop using him as your scapegoat. You said you were going to release him today, so release him."

Some of the soldiers began to protest, but Giles spoke over the top of them. "I never made any such promise, and even if I had, your precious husband has made that impossible. Or didn't you notice that he just killed a prominent senior soldier in front of half the city?"

"What, am I supposed to apologize?" asked Jonan insolently, but Scarlett silenced him with a glare.

"Enough, Jo," she said sharply, turning back to her cousin. "You really want to punish him for that? Did you not realize the man was about to kill me?"

"Yes," said Giles, sobering at once. "I did realize. I was horrified. His talk was treasonous, but I never would have guessed he was so far gone. The general will certainly want to hear of it."

Scarlett felt a ripple go around the soldiers present, some unidentifiable sense alerting her to their disdain. Surely Giles wasn't really oblivious to it—surely he didn't actually believe that one soldier had gone rogue, and these others had no part in whatever treachery he had been involved in? But if her cousin saw what she did, he made no sign of it, instead turning to Jonan, sincerity behind his suddenly stiff tone.

"It is unfortunate that you were unable to stop him any other way, but I must still thank you for stopping the man from attacking Scarlett."

"I don't want your thanks!" spat Jonan, incensed. "Do you think I defended my wife as a favor to you?"

"Apparently not, although I believe you owe me a favor," said Giles cuttingly, his politeness instantly evaporating. "I can hardly believe I trusted you to keep my cousin safe. What a fool I was to intervene on your behalf last time you were imprisoned. I would never have imagined what an advantage you would take of my generosity."

"I owe you nothing," Jonan returned. "You didn't do what you did for my sake. And I don't have to account to you for anything that's happened between me and Scarlett. You like to go on about 'your cousin', but as I recall you weren't willing to lift a finger to protect her from her father! I'm the one who kept her safe!"

"Is that so?" Giles laughed unpleasantly.

He stepped forward menacingly, glowering down at Jonan, who was at a distinct disadvantage with his arms still being held in a vise-like grip by the soldiers.

"Enough!" Scarlett cried, angrier than either of them. "You're behaving like children, both of you, and I will not be the excuse for your territorial dispute!"

"What she means," said Giles, never taking his eyes off Jonan, "is that you have the manners of a dog."

The soldiers jeered, and Jonan bristled.

"I think I know what she means better than—"

"What I mean," snapped Scarlett, more furious than ever, "is exactly what I said. Neither one of you speaks for me, so stop making fools of yourselves."

She might have saved her breath, because neither man paid the least attention to her speech.

"So you regret springing me last time, do you?" Jonan said to Giles. "Then I guess your pride is more important than your cousin, after all. You let me out because you wanted me to find Scarlett and keep her safe, and to stop a war. I did all three, but it seems that wasn't worth the cost of letting me live, and breathe your Balenan air. Well I don't care what you regret—I still say I owe you nothing. My only regret is being stupid enough to come back here and give you another chance to kill me, which is obviously what you wanted to do all along."

"Why did you come here?" snapped Giles. "No one wanted you to come."

"Why do you think?" Jonan shouted, getting agitated. "You think I wanted to come back to this accursed place? I came for

Scarlett! To make sure you didn't eat her alive for the crime of having more compassion than the rest of your filthy country put together!"

"*Is* that why you came?" asked Giles, apparently unaware of the angry mutter passing through the soldiers at Jonan's insult to Balenol. "From what I've been told, you came to make sure we didn't succeed in reminding her of how much better she could have done for herself."

"Stop it, Giles," said Scarlett sharply.

But she could see that the damage was already done. Jonan was looking between the two cousins, his look of betrayal making it clear that he had interpreted the comment just as Giles had wanted him to, and was now piecing together a very skewed version of the things Scarlett had said about him to Giles.

"If you didn't actually want me to find her," he said, his tone suddenly sulky rather than defiant, "then why *did* you let me out last time? You can't pretend you didn't know how I felt about her."

"Of course I wanted you to find her," said Giles sharply. "I wanted to be sure she was safe. But you told me you were a man of honor, and I believed you like a fool."

"What are you implying?" demanded Jonan furiously.

"I'm not *implying* anything!" Giles retorted. "I'm openly stating that a man of honor wouldn't have prevented her from coming home like you did."

"I didn't prevent her from—"

"Didn't you?" challenged Giles. "You're telling me you didn't insist on her marrying you before you'd let her come back here? Let me guess—you said it was so she'd be safe."

He leaned closer, but Scarlett still had no difficulty hearing his angry words. "I'm not so easily duped, *Jonan*. I know as well as you do that you wanted to pressure her into marrying you while she was far from her home and her family, with no other options, so that she wouldn't come to her senses and realize what a mistake it was!"

"It wasn't like that at all!" Scarlett cut in, stepping up to stand beside Giles, her fists balled. "No one pressured me, and I resent the suggestion that I'm easily duped!"

Again neither man looked at her, both breathing hard as they glared each other down. Scarlett had expected Jonan to have an angry retort of his own ready, but she thought he looked suddenly less mutinous and more unsettled. The sight filled her with a vague disquiet.

"I know you think you don't need anyone to look after you, Scarlett," said Giles, turning to her at last. "But even you can't deny that you were vulnerable over there in Kyona, all alone. You tell me Jonan saved your life, and of course I'm glad he did. But if he really had as much integrity as he claims, he would have brought you safely home, and sought the blessing of the head of your house to pursue you honestly."

"That would have been difficult," said Jonan belligerently, "since I had just run my sword through the man's heart. There was no head of her house to consult."

"Lord Wrendal seems to feel otherwise," Giles snapped. Jonan froze, his face showing nothing but shock, and Scarlett jumped in before his imagination could run too wild.

"He means Scanlon."

Jonan frowned at her, distracted for a moment from his argument with Giles. "Your brother? What does he have to do with it?"

Scarlett didn't immediately answer, her attention again drawn to the soldiers who were still grouped around them, listening keenly to every word. She was sure she hadn't imagined it. The rustle that had passed through the group at the mention of Scanlon had turned into a barely contained ripple of mirth at Jonan's question.

Giles took advantage of her silence to regain control of the conversation. "Of course you wouldn't think her own brother has any relevance to the question of her well-being. Enough. I have other things to do than stand here and argue with you. Especially now that you have probably undone all my previous efforts on your behalf. If I manage to get you out of Nohl alive, it won't be any thanks to you." He glared at Scarlett. "Or you, Scar. If you had let me arrange to have the marriage set aside, Jonan might even now be safely on his way back to Kyona."

"If you think," growled Jonan, "that I'm getting back on that ship without Scarlett—"

"I don't," said Giles curtly. "I think that short of something miraculous, you're not going anywhere, at least not in one piece. But you can't say I didn't try."

And Scarlett had to admit that he didn't look happy about Jonan's probable fate as he turned to the soldiers gripping Jonan's arms. "Return him to the dungeons, pending a decision by the crown."

He glared the soldiers down in turn. "And no more unsanctioned beatings. We are in the king's city, not the jungle. I will keep a closer eye on him this time, and I will personally ensure that anyone who perpetrates violence against him while he is in the royal dungeon will share whatever penalty the king decides to impose upon the prisoner."

The soldiers muttered and glanced at each other, but unlike their deceased leader, none of them were willing to openly challenge Giles and the crown he represented.

"Wait!" said Scarlett, as the soldiers began to move away, Jonan borne along in their midst. "I said wait!"

The soldiers ignored her, and Jonan wouldn't meet her eyes, his expression uncharacteristically subdued. She started after the group, but Giles's hand shot out, holding her back in a firm grip.

"Leave it be, Scarlett," he said grimly. "He's in enough trouble already, and frankly so are you. If we're lucky, everyone will focus on Jonan's little stunt and will forget that you were the first one to start attacking soldiers. Honestly, what were you thinking?"

"I was thinking that my husband was about to be flogged for no reason, and as usual you were too passive to intervene!" Scarlett shot back. "This isn't good enough, Giles. I want him released. You should be rewarding him for preventing that soldier from committing murder in the castle courtyard, not throwing him back in the dungeon."

"Scarlett." Giles's face was very grave. "You know I've been trying to help him, but he's made it all but impossible with this last offense. It's going to be almost too easy now for Scanlon to get him executed."

"Scanlon doesn't want him executed," said Scarlett quickly, but Giles just raised his eyebrows.

"I'm sure he told you that, Scarlett, but surely you're not that naive."

"No, he didn't—never mind," said Scarlett, still too worked up about Jonan's situation to want to get into her theories about Scanlon. "I'm going to talk to Jo."

"Scarlett, that's not a good—"

"I don't want to hear it, Giles," Scarlett cut him off. "I stayed away all day yesterday on your instructions, and it did more harm than good. And I don't trust you anymore when you tell me he'll be safe there. Maybe you're too blind to see it, but the crown is losing control of the soldiers."

"Of course I'm not blind," said Giles, nettled. "I'm the one who told you that the crown is in a precarious position. Public opinion is volatile at best. But the soldiers aren't going to disobey my direct order. Not now that the corrupt one has been... removed from the equation."

Scarlett followed Giles's gaze and barely repressed a shudder. As they spoke, the head soldier's body was indeed being removed from the courtyard by some of the soldiers formerly under his command. The looks on the men's faces as they glanced toward the prince and his disgraced cousin told Scarlett that they weren't going to let this go easily. She suspected that the incident was already being reported to whoever was really behind the deceased soldier's insubordination.

"You can't really believe that man was one corrupt soldier acting on his own impetus when he openly defied your authority, Giles," she said. "Aren't you concerned that he seemed to have no fear of any consequence from disobeying you?"

"I think he's more than paid for his insolence, Scarlett," said Giles.

But the thoughtful frown on her cousin's face suggested to Scarlett that he knew there was more to the incident than he was letting on. She didn't have the energy to argue with him about his decision not to share his thoughts with her. From long force of habit he was used to thinking of her as someone who would have no interest in military or strategic matters, and nothing to contribute. It must be hard for him to remember that her superficial persona had been an intentional facade. And any danger to the Balenan crown was his concern, after all. She had a more pressing problem to resolve.

"You're wrong about Jonan, you know," she said softly. "He didn't steal me away from better prospects. I'm the one who's lucky to be married to him. I've never met anyone else who I respect more, or who I would be happier with. And well before I ever met him, I was fully resolved not to marry any of the fools from the Balenan court who were pursuing me for my face, and my position."

Giles met her eyes, his expression giving nothing away. "And you're wrong about what happened," Scarlett continued. "Jonan didn't pressure me not to come back. I didn't want to come back, not straight away. I was afraid of what might happen to me now that people know about what I did in the resistance."

She could see that he wanted to interrupt, and she stopped him with an upraised hand. "Yes, Jonan was worried about my family trying to turn me against him, as well as about my safety. But I was just as concerned about that as he was. You claim that he pressured me, and being pressured was exactly what I was afraid of, but not from him. From you, and the rest of the family. And since the moment we got here, you've been validating that fear with every word you've said. You were even ready to annul my marriage without my consent!"

She took a deep breath. "This mess is my fault. I put off coming back for too long, because I was afraid. I realize now that was a mistake. It made you think I was ashamed of having married Jonan, or afraid of what you would think about my decision. Nothing could be further from the truth. If you still want any relationship with me, you have to accept the choices I've made, and you especially have to accept Jonan. Stop blaming him for the fact that I deceived you. Even if he was executed, I would return to Kyona, because it's my home now. But," her expression became fierce, "he's not going to be executed, because I won't allow it to happen." She held Giles's gaze. "Whatever I have to do."

CHAPTER NINE

Without giving him a chance to reply, she turned and began walking toward the dungeon. She paused for a moment as she saw her aunt hovering nearby, evidently having heard the last of Scarlett and Giles's conversation. Scarlett had forgotten that Aunt Mariska was present. She couldn't blame the older woman for failing to intervene in the recent crisis—not all Balenan noblewomen had taken it upon themselves to train in knife fighting after all—but she was glad her aunt had witnessed the confrontation, because Scarlett was done hiding.

The two women locked eyes briefly, but Scarlett didn't wait to see what her aunt thought about what she had done or said. She wanted to see Jonan, and she wasn't delaying any longer.

She swept into the castle, through the entryway, and down toward the dungeons without breaking stride. She pushed past a confused and nervous-looking royal guard in order to enter, and was unsurprised to discover a couple of soldiers still lingering in front of Jonan's cell, trying with their words to inflict the injury Giles had forbidden them from inflicting physically.

"What are you doing here?" one of them demanded rudely,

stepping forward to intercept her. "You're not supposed to be down here."

"I'm here to speak to my husband," said Scarlett with icy calm, fingering the hilt of the dagger that she still clutched in one hand. "So get out of my way, or I will force you to choose between being knifed by me, or killing me right now and facing the consequences."

The soldiers exchanged a glance, then, with one last appraising look at her face, retreated from the dungeon in disorder. Scarlett watched them go with narrowed eyes, turning back toward Jonan when she was satisfied that they had left.

He had been slouched against the wall in apparent nonchalance when she had entered, but had jumped up at sight of her and approached the bars, which he now gripped with both hands. Their eyes met, her face still hard from her showdown with the soldiers. For a moment Jonan was silent, then he broke into a grin.

"You're never more attractive than when you do that, in case you weren't aware."

She held his gaze for a moment longer then, without another word, strode purposefully forward, dropping the dagger to the stone floor with a clatter. She reached through the bars and grabbed the back of his head with one of her hands, winding her fingers through his hair as she pulled him toward her and pressed her lips against his. The cold metal of the bars seemed to sting her temples, but the fire that raced through her from Jonan's lips was more than worth it.

He reached for her, eagerly, his arms managing to twine around her waist despite their shortened reach. She kissed him fiercely, ferociously, pressing herself against the bars in silent defiance of the barrier that had so unjustly been placed between them.

Her heart was still pounding from the crisis in the courtyard, and the gesture was full of determination, with nothing of goodbye in it. She was not going to let him die. He returned her kiss with his usual enthusiasm, his lips moving passionately against hers as one hand reached up to her face, his fingertips traveling over her forehead, her nose, her cheekbones, as if reassuring himself of her familiar features. She could sense in his touch the same frustration and anxiety at their separation, the same relief mingled with fear at their reunion, that had been consuming her.

After a frenzied minute, Jonan seemed to master himself, pulling back and resting his forehead against hers through the gap in the bars.

"Curse these bars," he panted. "And happy anniversary." His voice was low and unsteady.

"I've missed you," Scarlett whispered. The hand still on her waist tightened in acknowledgment, but otherwise Jonan didn't respond.

The security of his well-known touch, the comfort of mutual silence, overset the last of her control. She felt an involuntary sob in her throat, and the next moment silent tears were coursing down her cheeks.

"Don't cry," Jonan soothed. "Everything is going to be fine."

"I'm so sorry, Jo," Scarlett sobbed. "This is all my fault. You were right—we never should have left home. I'm so sorry I forced you to come. I'll get you out of this mess, I swear."

"Don't be silly," said Jonan lightly, "this isn't your fault. And you didn't force me to do anything. I don't regret coming."

She pulled back at this outrageous comment, giving him a look. He was infuriatingly stubborn, but at least he had succeeded in stopping her tears, she supposed.

"What?" he said incorrigibly. "I'm starting to feel quite at home, really. Nice to be back in my old little corner of paradise."

She frowned. Looking around, she realized with a fresh

surge of anger that they had put him in the execution chamber this time.

"How dare they?" she cried. "Giles didn't tell them to put you here!"

Jonan shrugged. "Yeah, well, I get the sense that dear old Giles is not quite as in control as he thinks." His expression darkened. "Even though he made it clear that I can be executed for all he cares."

Scarlett sighed. "He has been trying to help us, Jonan, in his own misguided way."

"To help *you*," Jonan corrected. "Mainly to help you get away from me, from what I can tell."

"Jo..."

"Well, who can blame him?" said Jo, his tone bitter. "No one wants to see someone they care about stuck with a controlling, dishonest husband. And when you confirmed his suspicions that I was the one keeping you away for fear you'd have better options—"

"I never said that!" cried Scarlett, stung.

"I know you didn't," said Jonan, letting go of her and stepping away. "You're much too kind, and too loyal, to say anything of the sort."

At the loss of his touch, she felt suddenly cold, despite the humid air. Jo put his hands up to his head, looking more miserable than she had seen him in a long time. Somehow the gesture made him look younger and more vulnerable, the bruises on his face standing out clearly. She reached through the bars, only just able to reach him now that he had stepped back, and touched a hand gently to the cut above one eye.

"Oh, Jo," she whispered, tears standing in her eyes. "I wish I'd been there. I should never have let Giles convince me that you were safer if I stayed away. But I thought it was worth waiting the extra day if only so that it would be too late for the king to undo our marriage. Why did you let them beat you?"

Jonan closed his eyes at her touch, gripping the bars with one hand and leaning his head against it. "I didn't exactly *let* them. There were a lot of them, and I was bound, after all."

"But—" Scarlett glanced down at the rock on its chain around Jonan's neck. "You really couldn't fight them off? How many were there?"

Jonan shook his head, understanding her meaning perfectly. "I can't access the rock's power. It hasn't been working for me, except just then when I fought that soldier who was about to kill you."

Scarlett frowned over the unexpected information, trying to make sense of it. Looking up, she saw Jonan watching her closely, a wistful, almost longing look in his eyes.

"Don't worry, Jo," she said quickly. "We'll figure out what's causing the problem, like you figured out how to work it in the first place. Besides, you don't need it—you're strong enough and smart enough without it."

He shook his head. "It's not that. I'm not worried about the rock."

She waited, but for a long moment he was silent.

"Jo?" she prompted.

"I never meant to manipulate you, Scar." His voice was little more than a whisper.

"What?" she said, startled. "Of course you didn't. What are you talking about?"

"What Giles said," Jonan went on, his eyes pleading with hers. "I swear I didn't mean to—I never thought of it that way. I wanted to protect you, but maybe he's right. Maybe I also didn't want to risk you changing your mind. I mean...everyone in our community loves you so much, you fit so well, I forget you're not Kyonan. I didn't really think about what I was asking of you, what it means for you to leave all your people behind." He swallowed. "I can't stand the thought that maybe I did take advantage of your vulnerability, when you were there all alone."

"I wasn't alone," Scarlett choked out. "I was with you."

"That's exactly the point," said Jonan, looking more distressed than ever. "You had no one but me, and maybe it *was* the move of a scoundrel to tie you to me without coming back here, without including your family. I filled your head with my fears about your safety if we came back, but now that we're here, it's pretty clear I'm the problem, not you. Without me, everyone would be happy to welcome you back."

"That's not true!" said Scarlett quickly. "There are plenty of people who want me dead, too. Giles has been manipulating the situation to try to get the blame to fall on you instead of me." She scowled at the thought, but Jonan gave a strange little laugh.

"Well that's something, at least. Maybe I do owe him one after all." He met her eyes again, his expression anguished and unfamiliar. "I heard all about the banquet last night. And even seeing you in that dress..." He reached through the bars and touched her bare shoulder. The gesture was tentative, but even so it sent a tingle through her.

"It brings it all back so vividly, I hardly feel like you're mine anymore," Jonan went on. "Back then I thought nothing of your title and position. More than that, I despised it. But now I see what Cal and Elnora's lives are like...ours are so different. I didn't fully understand what you were throwing away for my sake. Maybe it would have been better for you if Giles had succeeded with his plan. Tell me truthfully, Scar. If Giles could fully clear you from blame, if I went back to Kyona and you stayed here, would you be happier than you are back in the forest?"

"Jo!" said Scarlett, aghast. "How can you even ask me that? I thought I told you not to let them get into your head! What on earth did those soldiers do to you?"

Jo shrugged. "I don't care about the beating, Scarlett, I really don't. But the way they talked...anyone would think you'd married an animal instead of someone from a different kingdom."

Scarlett's heart seemed to squeeze at the thought of Jonan being treated in such a way. But she wouldn't have expected him to be ruffled by it. "And why do you care what they say or think?" she demanded.

"I didn't at first," said Jo. "I laughed it off. But then you didn't come. I was so afraid for you, I thought you were locked up somewhere yourself, or worse. But then I heard all about the banquet, and..."

He trailed off, and Scarlett felt an agonized pang as she remembered the banquet, how she had greeted the king, been escorted to the meal by an eligible young nobleman, received the compliments of her persevering admirers, all with the appearance of contentment. Meanwhile Jonan had been beaten and taunted, locked in a dank prison cell. She felt suddenly sick at the thought. She had been polite instead of honest, falling back into her old habit of playing a part, and Jonan had paid the price. She had never imagined he would be so shaken by her absence.

"I'm so sorry, Jo," she whispered. "I didn't mean to hurt you." She swallowed, and her voice grew stronger. "Surely you don't really need me to tell you how I feel. You know I don't care about any of this nonsense. You know I'm happy with you."

Before Jonan could respond, they were both distracted by the sound of approaching footsteps. The royal guard who manned the prison came into view, looking stressed.

"You need to leave. No one cleared a visit to the prisoner, and you've been in here for far too long."

Scarlett stiffened. "We're in the middle of a conversation. I don't care if I have permission to be here or not."

"I'm sure you don't," said the guard dismissively. "But I'm answerable for this dungeon, and I do care. If I'm any judge of the mood out there, someone's going to lose their head, and I don't care for it to be me, understand? So get out."

Scarlett glared back at him, ready to make a scene, but Jonan stepped in. "He's right, Scarlett. The situation is already explosive, and we don't want to provoke anyone."

This entirely un-Jonan-like attitude alarmed Scarlett as much as his words had done a minute before. She started to protest, but he shook his head.

"Go, Scarlett. I'll be all right here for now."

She stared at him unhappily for a moment, while the guard hovered impatiently. There was no point lingering to talk to Jo if he didn't want to be talked to.

"Fine," she said, her tone communicating that she was giving in under protest.

There were so many things she wanted to say, but the guard's presence prevented any private conversation. With a final hard look at her husband, who still wore a defeated expression that looked out of place on his face, she swept out of the dungeon.

He might be defeated, but she wasn't. It was time to find out exactly who was behind this nightmare, and bring them down for good.

CHAPTER TEN

Scarlett marched straight to her room, determined to make one change before she did anything else. She rummaged through her trunk, throwing garments around heedlessly until she found what she was looking for. There.

A few minutes later, she surveyed herself in the looking glass and smiled grimly. If the Kyonan court dress had raised eyebrows, the close fitting green tunic and brown leggings that were customary in the Forest of Rune were going to be a scandal.

She started down the corridor, not sure where she was going, but in no doubt as to who she was looking for. If she wanted to get to the root of the problem, there was only one person to confront.

But she had barely gone five steps when she heard her name, and turned to see her aunt hurrying toward her.

"There you are, Scarlett! Are you all right? Where have you been since—" The flow of words ceased abruptly as Aunt Mariska took in Scarlett's change of outfit. The middle-aged princess had too much decorum to comment, but the same couldn't be said for her companion.

"Wow, Scar!" said the youngest of Scarlett's cousins, as he looked her up and down. "Is that what girls wear in Kyona?"

"Hey Roland," said Scarlett, not quite suppressing a grin. He had been only fourteen when she had left a year ago. But the way her cousin's eyes widened at the form-hugging attire told her that he had begun to appreciate girls differently since then. "Some of them do. The ones in the forest, where I live."

"Maybe I should go for a visit, too," said Roland, and her grin broadened.

"Roland," said Aunt Mariska, repressively. She turned to Scarlett. "Are you going to the audience chamber?"

"No, I—wait, why?" Scarlett asked, frowning. "What's happening?"

"Some of the court are up in arms about what happened this morning. They're petitioning the king to have Jonan executed."

Scarlett groaned. It wasn't exactly unexpected, but they certainly didn't waste any time. "I'm not going to let that happen, Aunt Mariska," she said grimly. "I know you don't like Jonan, but—"

"I don't dislike him," said Aunt Mariska quickly. "I simply don't know him. But I'm glad he makes you happy, and I don't want him to be executed."

"Thank you," said Scarlett quietly, ready to take small victories. "Who's leading the call for his execution?"

"One guess," snorted Roland, and Scarlett grimaced.

"Lord Grentan, I imagine." Neither one of them denied it. "And my brother?"

"Scanlon?" asked Roland, frowning. "No, I don't think he was even there when we left to come and find you."

Scarlett paused for a moment, torn. She wanted to hunt Scanlon down without delay, but it seemed she had little choice.

If the king was currently holding court on the issue of Jonan's fate, she needed to be there. Without further discussion, she took off toward the king's audience chamber, her aunt and cousin following behind her.

Her mind raced as quickly as her feet as she sped through the familiar halls. King Siloam was indolent, it was true, and easily persuaded by stronger wills. But surely he wouldn't order Jonan executed so hastily. Prince Rupert usually hovered nearby, ensuring that his brother didn't commit himself to any disastrous course. She would just need to persuade both Uncle Rupert and the king that executing Jonan would be an enormous mistake. The soldiers might not care that he was an emissary of the Kyonan king, but Prince Rupert certainly would.

However, it seemed that she was too late to sway the tide. As she approached the audience chamber, a stream of people began to exit, talking excitedly among themselves. She ignored the way most of them stared at her outlandish attire, pushing through the throng to enter the chamber and demand an explanation. But the king had apparently already left, and there was no sign of Uncle Rupert.

"What happened?" she asked a nearby page. "What was the decision?" But the boy just stared at her as if she was a visitation before scampering off to join the exiting crowd. She followed him back out into the corridor and caught a glimpse of Lord Grentan walking away with one of his cronies. He looked more self-satisfied than ever, and her heart sank.

"Scar, what did you find out?" Roland appeared unexpectedly at her elbow. "What did they decide? Are they going to, you know, slice off his—"

"I don't know," Scarlett interrupted her cousin in a curt voice, not needing him to finish his sentence any more than she needed the accompanying dramatic hand gesture to understand his meaning. "No one's left in there, and I didn't hear the outcome."

"Are you still looking for Scanlon?" Roland asked.

"Yes," said Scarlett quickly. "Did you see him?"

"Over there." Roland jerked his head back over his shoulder, indicating her brother. "Talking to the general in that opening."

Scarlett frowned as she followed his gaze to see Scanlon and the general conversing in a nearby doorway. Roland's choice of words triggered something in her mind. What had Scanlon said to the general last night, as she was walking away? That he would have his opening. His opening to do what—start a war with Kyona? If so, why didn't Scanlon want Jonan executed? Surely that was an easy road toward war.

"Thanks Roland," she said, striding through the crowd. The various knots of people were moving away from the audience chamber, so the area was all but deserted by the time Scarlett reached her brother. As the bustle subsided, her quick ears caught Scanlon's words before he was aware of her presence.

"Can't you control your own soldiers, curse you? Their little flogging exercise this morning has forced the issue much too soon."

The general's words were clipped and angry. "Watch yourself, My Lord. You may have come up with this plan, but as you've made very clear, I don't answer to you." He grunted. "I'll admit they were out of line. I underestimated how hated this Kyonan brat is."

"If the king goes through with this execution, it will ruin everything," Scanlon snapped. "This is exactly the show of strength we're trying to avoid."

The general didn't answer, his eyes sliding past Scanlon and narrowing as they settled on Scarlett. His companion turned quickly, following his gaze. To Scarlett's surprise, her brother looked pleased to see her, at least until he noticed her attire.

"Scarlett, have you no shame? You may as well walk about the castle naked!"

Scarlett scoffed. The clothes, although fitted to her shape, covered much more of her than any Balenan dress she had ever owned. There was something humorous about the fact that the dresses of Nohl would be considered just as outrageously improper in Kyona as her Kyonan attire was here. But this was hardly the moment for such reflections.

"I didn't come looking for you to talk about fashion, Scanlon," she said.

"Were you looking for me?" he asked, surprised. "How gratifying. I'm sure you'll be equally flattered to know that I was about to come looking for you." The inevitable sneer in his voice made the revelation anything but flattering, but Scarlett held her peace. "As it happens, you are exactly who we need. It seems we must form an alliance, my dear sister. Temporary, of course."

Alliance? Scarlett stared at him, several things clicking into place in her mind. The fact that Scanlon seemed to constantly be talking with the general, the reaction of the soldiers when Scanlon was mentioned that morning, the unusual insult used by both her brother and the soldier in the courtyard, almost as if they had been discussing Jonan together.

"You're working with the soldiers," she said slowly. "What are you up to, Scanlon, to form such an alliance? What interest do you have in common with the military?"

Scanlon's mocking smile faltered for the briefest moment, but his words were as smooth as ever. "What does it matter to you, my dear Scarlett? Much more to the point is the interest you and I now have in common. Are you aware that your *husband*—" his tone made the word into an insult— "has just been sentenced to be executed this very day?"

Scarlett sucked in a breath, her thoughts instantly distracted from her attempt to figure Scanlon out. "Today?" she gasped. "They're planning to execute him today?"

"So the king has just decreed," confirmed Scanlon lazily. He looked at her with interest. "I must say, you were conspicuously absent during the audience on the matter. Did the enterprising Lord Grentan manage to keep you away like he did our Uncle Rupert? Or can it be that your allegiance to your Kyonans is wavering?"

Scarlett ignored the bait, trying to grasp a nebulous thought sparked by Scanlon's talk of allegiance.

"Assuming you do still want to rescue your ill-bred husband, we have a common purpose, because I don't at all want to see him executed."

Scarlett frowned, her mistrust growing. "And since when are you so concerned for Jonan's welfare?" she asked. Her gaze passed to the general, who had taken no part in the conversation, and was still staring in disgust at her clothes. "What do either of you gain by saving his life?" She paused, remembering what she had overheard Scanlon saying just a minute before, that the execution would ruin everything. "Or is that the wrong question?" she said slowly. "Should I instead be asking what you would lose by him being executed? How would that make you lose your opening?"

Scanlon just smirked, but the general finally pulled his attention to her face, looking wary. She must be on the right track.

"Why do you want to avoid a show of strength?" Scarlett continued, her eyes flicking between them. "Why have you been riling everyone up if you don't want to provoke drastic action?" Their faces gave nothing away, but her thoughts flew suddenly to the now-dead soldier in the courtyard that morning, defying Giles's authority, and it all fell into place in her mind. "It's *your* allegiance that has changed," she said quickly. "And you're trying to bring the populace with you. You're riling people up to think that the crown owes them an execution, then counting on Giles's intervention to make sure the crown fails to deliver. They're so worked up, they might just be persuaded to think they need a change in leadership."

The general's expression was more guarded than ever, but Scanlon seemed unconcerned by her shrewdness. "But sadly, Giles's intervention seems not to have been sufficient. Which is where you come in, sister."

"As if I would ever help you!" Scarlett protested. "What are you thinking, anyway, Scanlon? Do you think if you can depose the royals, the people will turn to you as king? It's absurd!"

"Me?" laughed Scanlon. "I don't want to be king. As you have so beautifully illustrated with your unsuspected capacity to manipulate our dear departed father, much more can be achieved when standing just behind the one in power. Besides, who said anything about a king? As our current monarch has demonstrated," Scanlon's handsome features twisted in a sneer, "blue blood does not guarantee leadership ability. Perhaps it's time to move forward."

Scarlett's jaw dropped open as she stared between Scanlon and the general. "A military coup? You want to do away with the monarchy?"

"What are you doing?" muttered the general to Scanlon, but the younger man just shrugged.

"What, do you think she won't play her part if she knows our ultimate objective? I think she'll still do all she can to keep her precious little Kyonan alive. As to the rest—don't worry, no one will take her seriously. With one obvious exception, she's the most hated and least trusted person in this city."

Scarlett glared at him. "I want no part of your schemes, Scanlon."

He smiled maliciously back. "Well, I'll admit that my plans

will be disrupted by your husband's execution. So if you want to do me a mischief, by all means, sit back and do nothing to prevent it. I believe it's scheduled to occur within the hour."

Scarlett ground her teeth. Her brother had her right where he wanted her, and he knew it. He didn't have to make himself prominent by advocating for Jonan to be spared—he knew he could count on her to do whatever it took to prevent the crown from taking the violent action that would satisfy its bloodthirsty subjects. And little as she wanted to further his plans, what choice did she have? She would just have to focus on extricating Jonan, then deal with whatever was coming after.

She had no more time to waste on her infuriating brother. If it was true that the execution was scheduled to happen within the hour, every minute had become precious.

CHAPTER ELEVEN

Scarlett turned away from the two men and took off running, heading for the royal wing, determined to make someone listen to her, whatever Scanlon thought.

She came to a halt in front of what she knew to be a small but lavishly furnished receiving room. The presence of half a dozen royal guards outside the door told her that King Siloam was within. The door was open, but one of the guards stepped forward to intercept her progress, eyes narrowed.

"Halt. What is your business in this part of the castle?"

"I need to see the king," said Scarlett hastily.

The guards laughed unpleasantly. "I don't think so."

"But I have information he must know," Scarlett protested, knowing how weak the explanation sounded. She didn't think that the treachery of the military had extended to the royal guard, but without knowing for certain she didn't want to risk being more explicit.

"His Majesty is otherwise occupied," said one of the guards dismissively. And Scarlett could hear that this was true, at least. The door was open, and although from her angle she couldn't actually see the men within, she had no difficulty recognizing the voices issuing from it. She hovered, arguing half-heartedly with the guards while her sharp ears picked up the conversation in the room.

"What do you mean, immediately?!" Uncle Rupert spoke sharply. "I was gone for half an hour—how were you so quickly convinced to order an execution?!"

"I am sick to death of this Kyonan boy," said the king, sounding petulant. "He is all anyone petitions me about all day long, and I want to be done with him once and for all. You are just blinded by affection for your niece."

"That's nonsense," replied Uncle Rupert, and Scarlett had to agree. "My niece has nothing to do with this. The boy is here as an official emissary of his king."

"Everyone said that last time, and it turned out to be no such thing," said King Siloam, dismissively.

"But this time it is true, Siloam! If we kill him, it will be seen as an act of war."

"Lord Grentan doesn't seem to think so. He says that this King Calinnae will have to accept that the murder of one of our soldiers changes the situation. We could hardly let such an offense go unpunished."

"That is foolishness, brother." Prince Rupert sounded as frustrated as Scarlett felt. "Lord Grentan is pursuing his own agenda."

"Enough." The king's voice was uncharacteristically firm. "My mind is made up. I know you think me incapable of making my own decisions, but you're wrong. Now let's hear no more about it."

This statement was followed by silence, and Scarlett didn't realize that her uncle was taking leave of the king until he suddenly emerged from the room, pausing in surprise at the sight of her still facing off with the guards.

"Scarlett! What are you doing here?" His expression was hard, but she pushed on eagerly.

"Uncle Rupert, I need to see the king!"

"Dressed like that?" her uncle asked, looking her over with disfavor. "Absolutely not." He began to walk away from the receiving room, and Scarlett kept pace with him, abandoning her fruitless argument with the king's guards. Two of the guards followed Prince Rupert, walking a respectful distance behind them.

"Who cares what I'm wearing?" she said impatiently. "Uncle Rupert, trouble is brewing. There's a plan to—"

"I am well aware of what's being planned. I'm sure you wish to petition the king about your husband's execution, but believe me it will do no good. I don't want this execution any more than you do, and I've already spoken to him. Unfortunately, he is resolved. Even if he would see you, your meddling would only make matters worse."

"It's not just the execution," she said quickly. "It's Scanlon. He's—"

"I'm not interested, Scarlett," said her uncle, cutting her off ruthlessly. "You've made an almighty mess already, and you needn't look to me for help to get out of it. Any dispute between you and your brother is a domestic matter, and if you had more class, you would not wish to air it outside your own household."

"It's nothing to do with my household," Scarlett cried, frustrated. "It's yours! He's speaking treason, just listen to me!"

"Your husband has nothing to do with my household," said Prince Rupert brutally, pausing in the doorway to his personal chambers. "Dramatic allegations will not convince anyone, Scarlett, not when we are all now perfectly aware that you will do—and say—anything to protect your Kyonans. If you wish to pay your last respects to your husband, I suggest you stop wasting your time with me and go down to the dungeons." He entered his rooms as he spoke, closing the door behind him.

"Uncle!" Scarlett cried, but it was no use. The door remained shut, and the two guards now flanked it, their stony expressions making it clear that she would not be gaining entry.

Giles. She needed to find Giles. Surely he would listen to her. She took off running once again, her uncle's last words ringing in her ears and filling her with terror. How long had it been since the king's pronouncement? How long before it was too late? Should she abandon the attempt to tell the royals about Scanlon's treachery and go straight to the courtyard?

She wasn't even sure where to find Giles, so she redirected her steps back toward her own room. She ransacked her trunk again, concealing an extra two blades on her person. She then went through Jonan's trunk, which had somewhat ironically been brought from the ship to her chamber. She was hunting for a spare weapon, but she frowned when her foraging uncovered a document with the official seal of Kyona's king.

Her eyes widened as she scanned the parchment. This would have been extremely useful a day earlier, but she had never seen it before. Even in her anxiety for him, she couldn't help but roll her eyes at the absent Jonan. It was so like her husband to neglect to mention such a practical—and crucial—detail.

She tucked the parchment into her bodice, hoping desperately that it wasn't too late to use it. In addition, she strapped Jonan's spare sword belt around her slim waist. It was awkward and too large, but better than no sword at all. She could only assume that the sword he usually carried on him had been seized when they arrested him at the dock.

This task complete, she hurried toward the entranceway, reflecting that with all this running, it had been well worth changing out of her impractical dress. The need to choose between finding Giles and going straight to the courtyard was removed by her cousin's well-timed appearance as she hurtled toward the castle's front door.

"Giles!" she cried, seizing his arm.

"Scarlett! What in the kingdom are you wearing? Is that a *sword*?"

"Never mind, that's not important right now!" said Scarlett, exasperated.

"You're right," said Giles quickly. "Scarlett, I thought there would be more time, but the king—"

"I know, I know," Scarlett cut him off. "But there's something else happening, Giles. They're planning a coup!"

"What?" he asked, startled. "Who is?"

"The military," Scarlett said, stumbling over her words in her haste. "Scanlon. The general."

"Slow down," said Giles, looking bewildered.

Scarlett took a deep breath, willing herself to be more coherent. "Scanlon is working with the general, riling the people up so that when the crown fails to take aggressive action to satisfy everyone's anger, people will turn on the royals."

"But the crown *is* about to take aggressive action," said Giles blankly.

"Yes, well, I know that, but that wasn't part of his plan," Scarlett said impatiently. "He's counting on me to stop that."

"Whose plan?" Giles looked more bewildered than ever.

"Scanlon's! He's behind it."

"And he's counting on your help. You're in on it?" Giles raised an eyebrow.

"Of course not," snapped Scarlett. "But the fact that Scanlon doesn't want Jonan executed won't stop me from preventing the execution, and Scanlon knows that. He's using me, and I know he is, but what choice do I have?"

She knew she wasn't making much sense, and Giles's blank stare confirmed it.

"I'll be honest, Scar. I have no idea what you're talking about. I know some of the soldiers have been muttering, but it's a big leap from there to a coup. Let alone implicating the general himself. And what Scanlon has to do with any of it is beyond me. Where did you get all this information?"

"Scanlon told me himself! He and the general were talking after the king gave his verdict, and I overheard them, and he basically admitted that they're plotting against the crown!"

"Oh Scar," said Giles, the pity in his voice worse than his former confusion. "Scanlon has an ugly streak to him, there's no denying it. He knows how hard this is on you, and he was trying to bait you. I'm sure he would love to push you into making a fool of yourself, or worse—he probably wouldn't shed any tears if you got yourself executed alongside Jonan."

Scarlett went cold at the mention of Jonan's execution. She couldn't afford to waste time arguing with her cousin. "Giles, you have to help me stop the execution, then you have to root out whoever in the military is involved with this coup. They'll use any mercy the crown shows Jonan as the catalyst for an uprising. Giles!" she snapped, seeing that he was distracted by the scurry of people moving out of the entranceway toward the promised execution. "Why aren't you taking me seriously?"

Giles sighed. "Don't think I have no sympathy for you, Scarlett. I really do. I wanted to stop this, and I tried my best. But I failed. And forgive me for being skeptical when you then race in at the eleventh hour with some far-fetched tale about needing to stop Jonan's execution, or the fate of the kingdom will hang in the balance. I mean," he gave her a pointed look, "it wouldn't be the first time in the last twenty-four hours that you'd lied to me outright where Jonan is concerned, would it?"

"Look at my face, Giles!" Scarlett cried in desperation. "I

know I deceived you in the past, but you know me. Do you really think I'm lying to you right now? Plus, that doesn't even make sense. If I made the story up, why would I admit that sparing Jonan's life is exactly what the crown's enemies want?"

Giles frowned as he tried to keep up with the frenzied flow of words. "I don't think you're lying to me," he said at last, his voice quiet. "But I think Scanlon has been lying to you, trying to get into your head."

Scarlett growled in frustration. Why would no one listen to her? All she was trying to do was help Balenol, not that she had much reason anymore to wish the country well. Giles had said that everyone now knew of her secret activities as a rebel leader, but it didn't seem to have changed anyone's opinion that she was a foolish, gullible, vapid girl, not to be taken seriously. She could think of one person who would have listened to her warning, would have believed the sincerity and accuracy of her report without question. But he was currently being led out for execution, and not exactly in a position to help her in any attempt to thwart Scanlon.

"I don't have time for this," she said curtly. "Believe me or don't—it's your future crown on the line, what do I care if Scanlon topples the throne?" She tried to brush past Giles, but he grabbed her arm, stopping her momentum.

"Where are you going?" She could hear the genuine alarm in his voice. "I don't think you should go out there, Scarlett. It's not going to be pretty. You don't want to see it."

She stared at him in amazement. "You think my husband is going to be executed, and you expect me to hang back inside here to avoid seeing anything distressing? You have an even poorer opinion of me than I realized." Her eyes grew fierce. "Not that it matters, because there won't be anything distressing to see. I'm going to stop this."

"You can't stop it, Scar," said Giles, speaking softly even

while he continued to grip her arm firmly. "Don't put yourself through the agony of watching."

For a moment Scarlett's eyes glazed over, her mind going blank at the surreal nature of the moment. It was impossible not to call to mind the last execution she had witnessed before leaving Nohl. Or not quite witnessed, because she had been prevented from actually seeing Raldo beheaded, that time by Jonan himself. Jonan had held her in his arms, she remembered, for the first time. She had felt almost safe there, even then. He had let her cry against him, and unless she was mistaken, he had even shed tears of his own.

And now he was the one facing the blade.

She shook her head to clear it, wrenching her arm from Giles's grip at the same time. There had been too much at stake for her to throw off her disguise and rush to Raldo's aid when he was executed. But this time was different. She had nothing she was unwilling to lose in the cause of saving Jonan's life. She had no intention of hanging back, and no time to lose.

"Scar!" Giles cried as she pulled free of him. "The king has made up his mind—even my father couldn't convince him. You can't stop this!"

Scarlett paused for a moment on the threshold, turning back to meet Giles's eye with a steely expression.

"Watch me."

CHAPTER TWELVE

Scarlett's heart leaped into her throat as she stepped out into the courtyard. She had thought Jonan was still to be brought up from the dungeon, so the sight of him already standing at the base of the execution scaffold stopped her breath. What was wrong with Giles that he kept her talking when time was so crucial?

She ran through the crowd, shoving people aside in her haste to reach Jonan and the men surrounding him. She noticed that they were not soldiers this time, but members of the royal guard. Not that the soldiers were absent. She didn't have leisure to survey the eager crowd closely, but she did notice that a number of the people she pushed past wore the traditional military uniform. She was vaguely surprised that they were spread throughout the courtyard instead of standing in a block, but she didn't have time to puzzle over the matter. She had almost reached the front of the crowd when she saw a guard start to push Jonan toward the steps at the base of the scaffold.

"Stop!" she cried, but her voice was lost in the bustle. She shoved a middle-aged woman aside and burst out into the open space. "I said STOP!"

"Scarlett!" Jonan cried, mingled relief and alarm in his tone.

"Step back," said a guard, stepping forward to intercept her. His grip was firm, but his voice was kinder than that of the soldiers who had restrained her that morning. "Don't make a scene, now."

"I will absolutely make a scene!" Scarlett protested, making her voice as loud as possible. She could hear the excited murmuring of the crowd, and was confident she had their full attention. Good. She knew her Balenan people, and there was nothing they loved so much as a spectacle. And she was more than ready to make a spectacle of herself if that was what was needed.

"This man is an official foreign emissary, and I demand that you cease at once," she projected in a confident voice.

"We have our orders, My Lady," said the guard gruffly. "And they come from the king himself."

"Then I demand an audience with the king," said Scarlett boldly.

"I'm afraid that won't be possible," said the guard dryly. "He held an audience an hour ago, and this matter was settled then."

"I was not given the opportunity to be present!" said Scarlett. "And neither was he." She gestured toward Jonan. "Isn't it customary for those under accusation to have the chance to state their case before judgment is passed?"

The soldier shrugged. "That's not my area."

Scarlett looked around quickly and spotted a royal page, in dull green livery. She beckoned him forward, and he came readily, clearly as engrossed by the drama as the rest of the crowd.

"You would know about such matters," Scarlett appealed to him. "I'm right, aren't I? About the right of an accused to defend himself?"

"Well, yes, of course," said the page, "but not in the case of, you know..."

"Let's imagine I don't," said Scarlett, her voice dry. "Please enlighten me."

"Well, that law doesn't apply to sla—um, I mean Kyonans."

"Of course not," Jonan snorted, but Scarlett ignored him.

"But it does apply to foreign dignitaries, does it not? Even those from Kyona?"

"Ye-es," said the page hesitantly. "I believe so."

"It does," said Scarlett. "And I believe the law also states that foreign dignitaries are entitled to request an audience directly with the king over any matter pertaining to their kingdom, or a subject of that kingdom."

"Uh..." said the page, hesitating. Scarlett raised her eyebrows at him, and he shrugged apologetically. "I'm just a junior page, My Lady."

"She's right," said a voice behind her, and Scarlett turned. She hadn't even realized that Giles had followed her.

"Of course I am," she said crisply. "I was raised here at the castle, as everyone present is well aware." She looked at her cousin. "I was trained in the ways of the court alongside you, wasn't I, Your Highness?"

The look Giles gave her told her that he knew from the use of his title that she was not actually asking him so much as playing to her audience. But all he said was, "Indeed."

She turned back to the royal guards, satisfied. "This execution is unlawful. This man isn't a slave, and he has the right to answer any accusations against him."

"He's a Kyonan!" shouted a sudden voice from the crowd.

"That's right," Jonan yelled back unexpectedly. "And I'm proud to be Kyonan!"

Scarlett shot him an irritated look, but he raised an eyebrow, unrepentant.

"There you go," jeered an onlooker. "He's spoken in his own defense. Now let's have his head!"

"We don't need a trial," joined another random voice. "Kyona owes us blood!"

"Execute him!" Several voices joined the cry. Scarlett scowled at the crowd but couldn't identify the individual speakers.

"It's not for you to declare the execution unlawful, My Lady," said the guard in a measured tone. "The king has ordered it, and we are bound to obey."

"Then I invoke my status as a foreign dignitary to demand an audience with the king," she shouted over the melee.

"Foreign dignitary," scoffed another one of the guards. "You just said it yourself—you were raised right here in the castle."

"And who says this man is even a foreign dignitary?" chimed in the page, unexpectedly reasserting himself. "Didn't he claim to be an emissary of the king last time, when all along he was just an adventurer?"

"Adventurer," repeated Jonan, apparently pleased. "I quite like that."

"Be quiet, Jo," scolded Scarlett, once more glaring at him as she pulled the rolled parchment out of her bodice. He again raised his eyebrows at her, this time with quite a different expression, but she focused instead on the royal guard who had made himself a spokesman.

"I *am* a foreign dignitary," she declared, "and I can prove my status." She thrust the paper at the guard, who shrugged.

"I can't read," he said.

The page raced forward eagerly, leaning over the guard's shoulder. Giles moved forward in a much more dignified way and also began to read the parchment. He reached the end quickly, and looked up at Scarlett, his expression exasperated.

"You produce this *now*?"

"I didn't know about it before," said Scarlett impatiently. "Apparently Jonan forgot to mention it."

"What did I forget?" said Jonan, looking at the document more closely. "Oh, that." He saw Scarlett's look and shrugged defensively. "What? How was I supposed to know to mention it? Since when has our status been in question? I assumed they knew but just didn't care."

Giles grimaced, the expression seeming to acknowledge that it wasn't an entirely unreasonable conclusion to draw.

"Wait a minute," Jonan said suddenly, and everyone's eyes jumped to him. "You went through my trunk?"

"Yes," said Scarlett, staring at him in confusion. "What's the problem?"

"Your anniversary present was hidden in there," said Jonan, aggrieved.

Scarlett just rolled her eyes, not missing the look of utter disbelief on Giles's face. Her cousin didn't know Jonan, but she had long since ceased to be surprised at his tendency not to take anything seriously.

"Well, unless it's this sword," she said sarcastically, "It's still in there."

"What does the parchment say?" asked the guard impatiently.

"It's an official proclamation of King Calinnae of Kyona," said the page importantly. "That's his royal seal at the bottom, I believe?" He turned the statement into a question, looking to Giles for confirmation.

"Yes," Giles agreed. "That's the royal Kyonan seal."

"And it says that—"

"Louder!" shouted someone from the crowd, and the page cleared his throat importantly.

"It says, 'I, King Calinnae of Kyona, appoint the bearer of this document, Jonan of Nerita, and his wife Scarlett, as official representatives of the Kyonan crown for the duration of their state visit to the kingdom of Balenol. Jonan bears my authority to treat with the Balenan crown on matters pertaining to Kyona. Should he consider it necessary, he—or in his absence, his wife—has authority to make decisions regarding trade and relations between the two kingdoms...'"

The page trailed off, glancing up at the agitated crowd.

"You missed some," said Scarlett, her voice hard. "Finish the sentence."

The page looked uncertainly at Giles, but the prince said nothing, so the page cleared his throat and tried again.

"'—authority to make decisions regarding trade and relations between the two kingdoms, including authority to declare war.'"

The crowd had been silent while he read, but a muttering started to spread after these words. Scarlett saw uneasiness on many faces at the mention of war. People seemed to be looking at Jonan with new eyes, and no one more so than Giles. She perfectly understood the appraising look of surprise her cousin was directing at Jonan. The decision to give the status of royal representative to someone outside the court was unprecedented in Balenol, and probably in Kyona too. The authorization was a compelling statement of King Calinnae's trust in Jonan, and the delegation of the ability to declare war was unusual and dramatic. She could only assume that Cal had included that statement in an effort to protect her and Jonan from exactly what had happened.

"He can't declare war if his head has been chopped off," called someone from the crowd.

"But his wife still can," chimed in someone else, nervously.

Scarlett smiled in secret satisfaction. She knew it was silly to be pleased by such a thing at this moment, but it was the first time since arriving in Nohl that anyone had referred to her as Jonan's wife.

"So execute both of them," muttered someone near the front in an audible aside.

Jonan glared at the man aggressively, taking a step forward, which immediately caused the royal guards to swarm around him. Scarlett decided it was time to step in.

"Are you really going to deny my formal petition for an audience with King Siloam?" she asked the guard, who was clearly wavering.

"Of course not," Giles spoke for him. "The law must be upheld. You are quite right to remind us of your entitlement as a foreign dignitary." He turned to the page. "Carry this message to His Majesty at once: His Highness Prince Giles wishes to inform him that our visiting emissaries have requested a formal audience on the matter of the intended execution."

The page scurried off, and a restless muttering filled the courtyard as everyone resigned themselves impatiently to wait. Scarlett met Jonan's eye, and despite the tension of the moment, she couldn't help a small smile at the warmth in his expression.

"For a minute I thought I wasn't going to see you again," he said, his voice soft despite his evident attempt to keep his tone light. "I couldn't help wishing I could have another go at my last words to you."

Scarlett could sense Giles's curiosity, but she felt no need to enlighten him about her earlier conversation with Jonan, and how much Giles's unjust words had rattled her normally imperturbable husband. She moved forward, intending to stand beside Jonan, but the outspoken guard stepped between them, shaking his head.

"Until I hear otherwise, this man is still scheduled for execution. Stay where you are."

Scarlett scowled, but did as she was told. The guard could say what he liked, but surely they couldn't execute Jonan now. In light of the parchment she had produced, King Siloam would have to be out of his mind to hold to his belief that they could kill Jonan without provoking war. The crowd would be all the angrier for being so close to satisfaction before having their sport denied them, but that was neither her fault nor her problem.

She did feel a twinge of uneasiness that, in thwarting the execution, she was doing exactly what Scanlon wanted her to do. She scanned the crowd, but although she could still see quite a number of soldiers dotted throughout the courtyard, there was no sign either of her brother or the general.

Like everyone else, she was watching the entrance to the castle, expecting the page to reappear and summon all interested parties to the king's audience chamber. But no one had yet emerged when she heard Giles give a barely audible sigh. She turned to him in surprise, and saw that he was not looking across at the castle's entrance, but up at its walls. He quickly schooled his features, his long-suffering look giving way to a respectfully impassive face, but following his gaze, she understood what had exasperated him.

King Siloam, as lazy as ever, apparently did not intend to hold court in his audience chamber a second time that day. His personal receiving room had been built with a balcony overlooking the castle courtyard. Its purpose was to facilitate public addresses by the monarch, and to allow him to preside over other events and festivities. It had undoubtedly also been used in the past to allow the sovereign to see his judgments carried out via whipping or execution, but Scarlett had never seen King Siloam use it for such a purpose. He lacked the bloodthirstiness of her late father, and was happy to let others put his carelessly applied penalties into effect without his presence.

The crowd became aware of the king a moment after Scarlett had, and an expectant silence fell as everyone bowed. Scarlett saw Jonan turn, confused, to look behind him, and saw his eyebrow rise in astonishment at the spectacle. She cringed for her monarch. He looked quite pleased with himself, probably thinking that he had not only gotten out of extra effort, but that he made an imposing picture, stationed above his people in the ornate purple robe he wore for public audiences. In reality—at least in Scarlett's opinion—he looked foolish, lazy and out of place, as if he had no idea that an execution was underway.

For a moment there was silence, many people looking to Giles, apparently expecting him to take charge of the situation. But Scarlett could see at a glance that her cousin was reluctant to demean himself by shouting up at the balcony above, and she couldn't really blame him.

"Thank you Your Majesty," she called in a respectful tone, resigning herself to looking a little ridiculous, "for so graciously granting my request for an audience."

Jonan snorted derisively at her words, but Scarlett ignored him. Seeing that she had the king's attention, she started to curtsy before suddenly realizing that she was wearing leggings, and executing a low bow instead. King Siloam stared at her in open amazement, and she doubted he heard a word of her succinct but forceful explanation of the state of affairs.

But the page had clearly explained the matter to the king. When Scarlett was finished, he turned to his nephew, his voice carrying clearly across the courtyard due to the acoustics created by the balcony's clever design.

"Are you satisfied as to the authenticity of the document, Giles?"

"Yes, Your Majesty," said Giles calmly. "There can be no doubt that it is genuine."

"Well, well," said the king, a little displeased as he looked at Jonan. "I suppose we must release him, then."

The guards instantly obeyed, and Jonan shook out his limbs pointedly as the king continued, addressing the former prisoner.

"This matter has not been handled at all to my satisfaction, and you have certainly not been forthright. For the sake of your king I will show lenience, but I trust you will curb your violence in future. We are a civilized people here in Balenol, and we will not countenance the aggressive behavior that may pass as acceptable in Kyona."

Scarlett knew a moment of dread as Jonan opened his mouth to reply, but fortunately his inevitable disrespect was forestalled by an angry voice from the crowd.

"You're going to let him go?!"

Giles turned his head sharply, clearly trying to identify the speaker who dared to speak out so publicly against the king.

"You are weak!"

"You let the Kyonans leave, and now you let them walk all over us from afar!"

Scarlett sucked in a breath as additional voices swelled the chorus. Giles looked genuinely shocked by now, such open defiance against the crown being unprecedented. But Scarlett had expected something of this nature. She had given the military its opening, after all. As voices continued to call at random from the crowd, their sources difficult to locate, she suddenly understood why the soldiers had been spread indiscriminately throughout the space.

She opened her mouth to tell Giles that they needed to find Scanlon and the general, neither of whom was in sight. But all that came out was a startled squeak as she was unexpectedly grabbed by the arm and hauled toward the edge of the courtyard.

CHAPTER THIRTEEN

Scarlett had a dagger out so fast that she could only be grateful that the familiar voice penetrated to her consciousness before she could plunge it in anywhere.

"Easy, Scar! If you wanted to do away with me, it would have been much easier just to let them execute me."

"What are you doing, Jo?" Scarlett gasped, her heart jumping unevenly at how close her blade had come to Jonan's arm before she pulled her hand back with a start.

"Getting out of here, what else?" responded Jonan, still tugging her along. "My experience tells me that we've only got a short break before someone tries to kill one or both of us again."

They had almost reached the edge of the courtyard, but as if to prove the truth of his words, they found their way barred by a small knot of angry-looking civilians.

"Not so fast, Kyonan," one of them growled. "We don't care what papers your little king sent with you."

"He's actually quite tall," said Jonan conversationally, as usual seeming to feel no dismay at being outnumbered and unarmed. At least these townspeople also seemed to be carrying no weapons.

"Let us pass," demanded Scarlett furiously. "You heard the verdict. Are you going to defy the king?"

"Maybe it's about time," one of the men muttered, and Scarlett frowned. Scanlon and his allies had done their work well, it seemed.

"Our quarrel isn't with you," another man said to her, his eyes flicking back to Jonan. "It's Kyonan blood we want."

"Speak for yourself," snarled another. "She's thrown in her lot with them now. And for all the big talk of trade deals and alliances, I don't see any sign of Kyonan dragons coming to help us. She was planning to betray her own people all along."

Jonan bristled as several pairs of eyes turned aggressively toward Scarlett. She looked back to the front of the courtyard, wondering why no one seemed interested in the unsanctioned violence being threatened. She could see at a glance that the soldiers were succeeding far too well at riling up the crowd, and she was suddenly afraid for Giles, who was trying single-handedly to contain the impending eruption, his every line rigid with fury at the sudden mutiny. He needed backup, and quickly.

"I don't know," jeered one of the townspeople, his words slurring as if he was tipsy, despite the early hour. Scarlett turned back to her own confrontation to find that the man's eyes were fixed unpleasantly on her. "Seems to me it would be a waste to kill her now we know the ravishing Lady Wrendal is willing to debase herself outside her high and mighty class."

Her eyes narrowed, and she raised her blade, relishing the fact that she no longer had to play the part of the haughty but helpless peeress when men leered at her. But she had no opportunity to show off her skills. She felt Jonan stiffen beside her at the suggestive words, and as soon as the man stepped toward Scarlett, Jonan broke on the group like an enraged jaguar. He had obviously rediscovered how to access his hidden power, because he needed no weapon as he fell upon the aggressors.

In moments, four men were on the ground, either unconscious or too dazed to rise, and several more had taken flight. As soon as the coast was clear, Jonan once again seized her hand and began to run. Her protests fell on deaf ears, and in light of the many hostile pairs of eyes still trained on them, she allowed him to pull her along until they had left the courtyard.

Once they had wound through a couple of backstreets, however, she pulled Jonan to a stop, to his obvious reluctance.

"What was that?" she demanded, raising her eyebrows at Jonan, who was still glowering back toward the courtyard.

He stared at her blankly, his chest still heaving. "What do you mean? Did you expect me to stand by while they—"

"Of course not," she said impatiently. "But you didn't want to let me take even one of them?" She spoke dryly, and he flashed her a sudden grin.

"Sorry, Scarlett. But to be fair, I've been locked up since the moment we got here, and I think I needed the release more than you."

She shook her head, privately thinking he was right. Plus it was probably for the best. Aggressive as the men had been, it wouldn't have felt right to use her weapon against their fists.

"Come on," said Jonan, seeming to have caught his breath. "Let's go."

"Where?" asked Scarlett, nonplussed.

"Home!" said Jonan, as if it was obvious. "We can be at the ship in half an hour if we run."

"We can't just leave," said Scarlett, scandalized. "They have a crisis on their hands."

"Good," said Jonan fervently. "They'll be too distracted to realize we're gone until it's too late. Do you think I want to stay to go for round three in the dungeons? I wasn't kidding about the rats, Scar!"

"You don't understand, Jonan," said Scarlett quickly.

"Scanlon is planning a coup, with the general. I don't know how many of the soldiers are in on it, but they were intending to use the fact that the crown spared you from execution as the basis of an uprising. They want to topple the monarchy altogether."

Jonan stared at her for a moment, his mouth open.

"You believe me, don't you?" said Scarlett anxiously.

"What?" Jonan's expression went from amazement to confusion. "Of course I believe you." He smiled admiringly. "I was going to say that I'm impressed you managed to uncover a plot of this magnitude in such a short time, but I'm not exactly surprised. You've always been the sharpest person in the Balenan court, if they only knew it."

Warmth spread through her at his praise. His confidence was a balm after her frustrating attempts to warn the royals of the disaster hanging over them. But the pleasant feeling soon fled as she remembered Giles, facing off against the angry crowd.

"We need to find Scanlon," she said. "And the general. Neither of them were there in the courtyard, although it was definitely their soldiers working everyone up, and it makes me uneasy not knowing where they are."

She started back toward the courtyard, but Jonan caught her hand. "Why is this our problem?" he asked quickly. "Why didn't you just warn Giles?"

"I did," said Scarlett darkly. "But he didn't take me seriously."

Jonan shrugged. "His mistake, then. No reason to risk your life showing him you were right."

"It's not about being right, Jonan," said Scarlett quickly. "I can't help but feel partly responsible. The reason Giles didn't believe me was because I already lied to him yesterday. Plus, I played a part in Scanlon's plot myself, by stopping the execution."

"You mean *my* execution," said Jonan dryly. "I don't think

you can blame yourself for not letting your husband die just to delay some plot against the country that has basically disowned you."

Scarlett winced slightly at his words, and Jonan clearly saw it, looking instantly penitent. "Scarlett, I didn't mean—"

She cut him off with a wave. "Of course I don't blame myself for saving you, but it still irks me to know that Scanlon is going to use my actions to cause mischief."

"I can understand that," said Jonan, more gently. "But that doesn't make this our fight."

"Since when do you run from a fight?" Scarlett challenged, her eyebrows raised.

Jonan stepped forward with a sigh, closing the distance between them and running his hand through her hair as she looked up into his face.

"Since I have something very precious to lose," he said, and she threw herself hastily forward. His arms closed around her, holding her firmly against his chest, and for a brief moment they stayed that way. Scarlett could feel that, like her, Jonan's every muscle remained tensed, but she could also sense the mutual relief at being reunited.

"I know they've broken faith, Jo," she said, her voice muffled against his tunic. "But I can't just leave them to whatever Scanlon is planning without at least trying to help."

"I know," sighed Jonan, clearly already resigned to her answer. "And I can't criticize you for being so unselfish, when it's one of the things I most love you for. But I can't help wishing I could get you out of here right now, when we can still escape with our lives."

"I'm sure you'll be fine," said Scarlett bracingly. "You seem to have found your strength again."

"It's not me I'm worried about," said Jonan, leaning his forehead against hers. "But you're right, I figured the rock out almost as soon as you left this morning."

The growing sounds of strife in the nearby courtyard made Scarlett want to hurry back without delay, but she forced herself to be patient as Jonan took a deep breath. He clearly needed to get this out, whatever it was.

"Giles was right," he said, his tone uncharacteristically reserved. "I was selfish, and a little bit dishonorable even, to encourage you to stay away from your home until I'd locked you down."

"Jonan!"

"I'm not saying we shouldn't have done it," said Jonan quickly. "Just that my motivations weren't quite as good as I thought they were. And the power of the rock comes from putting your own interests last. It's no wonder it hasn't worked for me while we've been here. I told myself I was thinking of you —and I *was* trying to keep you from harm. But at heart I was thinking about myself, thinking how I could stop you from being influenced against me."

"You should have trusted me not to let that happen," said Scarlett quietly, moved by his confession.

"I know I should have," said Jonan heavily. "And that's my point. I should have put my fears aside and thought about what you actually wanted. I knew you were longing to see your family. And it wasn't exactly a secret to me that you were as nervous about how I would act as about how they would receive you."

Scarlett gave a small, unsteady laugh. Once again he was more perceptive than she gave him credit for.

"Giles thinks you made a bad choice," Jonan continued, "and I have to admit I haven't been as good a husband as you deserve. I would have been well served if you had shipped me back to Kyona and stayed here."

"Jo—" Scarlett protested, her feeling of panic from the dungeon returning, but he cut her off.

"*But*, I intend to improve," Jonan pushed on, smiling slightly at her alarm. "That's why we got married, isn't it? I'm supposed to have the rest of our lives to get better at putting you first. So I don't care whether it would serve me right, I'm not going home without my wife."

Scarlett beamed up at him, pleased to have the Jonan she knew back.

Jonan gave her a squeeze, his face suddenly fierce. "If I die here, so be it—you can add my name to the wall underneath Raldo's. But nothing will induce me to leave without you."

"Oh Jo," said Scarlett, her smile instantly disappearing in favor of an exasperated expression as she stepped back, unimpressed. This was the Jonan she knew, all right. "I think that blasted rock with its ridiculous formula for power has addled your mind. You do realize that it's possible to be determined to do something without resolving to die in the attempt, don't you?"

He grinned. "But where's the fun in that?"

She turned away from him, shaking her head indulgently. "If we're done with the theatrics, can we go now? Hopefully it's not too late after all your soul-searching confessions."

"Just one more thing first," said Jonan quickly, and she turned to him inquiringly.

"What?"

"Just in case," he said by way of explanation, then he pulled her suddenly back toward him and pressed his lips crushingly to hers. She melted against him instantly, their bodies pressed together much more satisfyingly than during their last kiss as Jonan's lips devoured hers briefly but passionately.

"Much better without the bars," he breathed when he pulled back, his thoughts obviously going in the same direction.

"Much better," Scarlett agreed, and Jonan grinned at her dazed expression.

"Ready?" he asked, as if they were going for a stroll through the jungle. Pulling herself together, Scarlett nodded.

"Then give me my sword, and let's go stop this coup."

CHAPTER FOURTEEN

Scarlett naturally took the lead, sprinting through the streets in a wide arc in order to come at the courtyard from a different direction. It felt almost dreamlike, running through the well-known streets, free of her restricting skirts, Jonan following behind her. It was both strange and familiar. They had done the same thing before, but never in daylight.

They were close to their destination when Scarlett heard a familiar voice, its curt orders cutting through the commotion of the nearby square. She threw out an arm, and Jonan careened to a stop beside her.

"Excellent, I see that Prince Rupert has arrived. Take half a dozen men, and secure the princess and the two younger sons."

Peering around the edge of a building, Scarlett saw a soldier hurrying away from her brother, who skulked in a side alley where he could see the courtyard but not be seen by most of the crowd filling it.

"You're a snake, Scanlon," said Scarlett without preamble, striding out from her hiding place now that her brother was alone.

He turned abruptly, his eyes passing briefly from her to Jonan and back again, his expression as self-satisfied as ever.

"Ah, my darling sister," he said in mock affection. "I wondered where you'd gotten to. I didn't want you to slip away before I had the chance to thank you for your help. You played your part beautifully." His smile grew as she glared at him. "Truly, I couldn't have done it without you. A brilliant performance."

Scarlett ignored the jibe. "Tell me you're not planning to kill Aunt Mariska and the boys."

He shrugged. "Only if it's necessary."

"How could you even consider it, Scanlon?" Scarlett protested. "She's our mother's sister! And Roland is little more than a child."

Scanlon's expression turned slightly sour. "From what I understand, our young cousin is older than you were when you started your little slave rebellion, so don't try to tell me he's a child. And the princess's connection to our mother is hardly a source of affection as far as I'm concerned. You might be our mother's likeness," he eyed her up and down scornfully, "but I take after our father, thank heaven." His eyes flicked to Jonan. "Which reminds me—I may not be prone to family affection, but I still owe retribution to my father's killer."

Jonan raised an eyebrow. "You would rather he'd succeeded in killing Scarlett, would you?"

"Infinitely," said Scanlon calmly.

"You really are like him," growled Jonan. "I'll admit, I was curious to meet my brother-in-law, but I can't say you make a good first impression."

Scanlon hissed, instantly taking offense at Jonan's familiarity. "I am no relation of yours, mongrel," he spat. "Just because my sister has degraded herself to become your harlot doesn't mean I will acknowledge you as—"

The insult was destined to remain unfinished, Scanlon's thought broken off by the sudden impact of Jonan's fist smashing into his face. The motion had been so swift that Scarlett could only gasp as her brother dropped heavily to the flagstones. She waited for a moment, but it quickly became clear he was unconscious.

"I *really* don't like your brother," said Jonan, trying to speak lightly, but betrayed by the rapid rise and fall of his chest, and the angry glint in his eyes.

"Neither do I," said Scarlett accusingly, "but you don't see me punching him in the face every time he says something rude. I think you broke his nose, Jo."

"I hope I did," said Jonan savagely, massaging his fist.

"Well, there's no time to worry about it now," said Scarlett, dismissing her brother from her mind and her sight as she hurried forward, seeking a better vantage point into the courtyard. Jonan followed, resisting with difficulty the urge to kick the unconscious Scanlon on the way past, if Scarlett was any judge of his body language.

The sight that met her eyes was more than enough to occupy her full attention. She heard Jonan's low whistle as he drew alongside her, but neither said a word. The courtyard was a writhing mass of people, shouting, stamping, and generally fighting each other. Some looked terrified, but many seemed to be hyped up by the unexpected opportunity to vent some of their frustration and resentment against the royals.

King Siloam was still safely up on his balcony, looking down with more astonishment than alarm at the seething crowd of people below. But Giles was in the thick of the fight, under attack from a number of burly men who were dressed as townspeople but held themselves suspiciously like soldiers. Scarlett's heart sank. How many of the general's traitors were spread throughout the crowd, posing as civilians, in addition to the uniformed soldiers she could see? Of course they would want it to seem like a people's uprising rather than solely a military attack against the crown.

The members of the royal guard who had been about to carry out Jonan's execution were fighting furiously, attempting to protect the prince, but they were dropping steadily. Glancing across the area, Scarlett saw Uncle Rupert, trying to reach his son, his sword weaving through the melee with a skill and energy at odds with his age and dignified bearing.

The sight of her uncle brought Scanlon's words back to Scarlett with a sudden rush. Her eyes swept toward the entrance to the castle, and she gasped as she recognized the soldier to whom her brother had issued his order. He had apparently succeeded in gathering several other soldiers, but had found his passage to the castle barred by a group of royal guards.

"Jonan," said Scarlett sharply, gesturing toward the fight with her head. "We can't let them get to my aunt and the boys."

Jonan followed her gaze and gave a curt nod, not needing her to explain. He met her eye briefly, the look passing between them communicating more clearly than words the mutual anxiety for one another that wound inextricably through their determination. Then Jonan took off, his sword already in his hand as he skirted the edge of the courtyard, heading straight for the fight at the castle's entrance.

Scarlett didn't stay to watch his progress, instead plunging into the crowd, bent on reaching Giles. Her progress wasn't as impeded as she expected, a slim young woman being ignored by the fighters where a sword-wielding man like Jonan would have been mobbed.

She no longer had a sword, a weapon she wasn't very proficient with anyway, so she knew she had to fight smart in order to make her dagger effective against the soldiers. The enraged townspeople were a different matter, as they were generally armed only with makeshift weapons, if at all. The king's well-trained royal guard would make short work of this mob, but the coup had been planned well, violence erupting so suddenly that the royals had very few of their own guards on hand.

Scarlett slashed her way through any challengers where necessary, leaving a trail of superficial injuries behind her. But it wasn't until she approached Giles's position that she really began to fight in earnest. Ducking and weaving, she came at the soldiers from behind while they were focused on the prince and his guards. Her blade flashed out and back again, stinging the unsuspecting soldiers like the giant black bees that were the terror of unwary wanderers in the nearby jungle.

Scarlett hadn't lied to her cousin when she said she didn't regret having killed people in her efforts with the resistance, but she had never relished it, and she worked hard to incapacitate without taking life wherever possible. One after another, soldiers fell back from the attack against the prince and his guards, sword arms maimed, the backs of knees stabbed, or shoulders pierced. In the general chaos, most of them had no idea what had taken down their fellows until they felt the steel of her blade themselves. But unlike his attackers, Giles did not have his back to her, and she saw her cousin's eyes grow round as he saw what she was doing.

She reached him eventually, the steady onslaught of soldiers slowing for a moment, and the surviving guards formed a semicircle in front of the pair.

"Scarlett," Giles said, panting from his recent exertions. "Thank you—for...for..."

Scarlett just nodded curtly, her face set and her eyes scanning the area for further threats. She was once again the confident rebel leader—a person Giles had never known.

Her eyes flicked to her cousin after a moment, and she raised an eyebrow at his stunned expression.

"What?"

"You just...I mean, I know you said, but...I wasn't quite prepared for seeing it myself."

She just shrugged, not sure whether to feel pleased or embarrassed.

"Where did you learn to fight like that?" Giles persisted. "Did Jonan teach you?"

"Jonan?" said Scarlett, surprised into an involuntary laugh. "Hardly."

Giles looked more confused than ever, and she smiled in spite of herself. "It was more the other way around. He's trained very hard this last year, but...don't tell him I said this, but I'm pretty sure I could still beat him in a knife fight. Swords, on the other hand, are an entirely different matter. Jonan is deadly with a sword."

She searched the chaos for him as she spoke, Giles following her gaze. She located him, at the edge of the courtyard, and her heart swelled with a rush of equal parts pride and fear at the sight of him living up to her claim. She thought that even Giles, an excellent swordsman, looked impressed at the way Jonan was cutting down all opposition.

She felt a surge of satisfaction, knowing that her husband showed to advantage in a crisis. Giles undoubtedly thought Jonan reckless and foolish, but even he would have to admire Jo's calm head as he managed to skillfully evade the royal guards who periodically came at him—evidently confused about his role in the fight—and focus his attacks instead on the treasonous soldiers.

"He's coming back into the courtyard," she commented suddenly. "That means he must have succeeded in stopping them. He went to take down a group of soldiers who were going after your mother and brothers," she explained in response to Giles's questioning look. "We heard Scanlon give the order ourselves, and Jonan didn't hesitate to go after them."

Giles's eyes widened in horror at the mention of his family, and Scarlett made no effort to keep the accusatory note out of her voice, remembering how little reason any of them had given Jonan to care about their safety.

But she didn't have leisure to watch her husband for long. Jo seemed to feel her gaze, and he looked up suddenly, his eyes locking on hers briefly before they passed to something behind her and widened in alarm.

Scarlett spun around to find that one of the plain-dressed soldiers had taken advantage of their distraction to come around the side of the guards' protective semicircle. He raised a well-polished sword—compelling evidence that he was not really a civilian—and Scarlett threw herself out of the way only just in time to evade his thrust.

She dropped into a fighting crouch, looking for an opening to make her smaller blade work for her, but before she had time to act, Giles had engaged the man sword to sword. She hung back, knowing she would only do more damage underfoot. It was clear that Giles was the better fighter, anyway.

"Scarlett!" She turned quickly at the sound of Jonan's voice and saw him running toward her. The guards protecting her and Giles seemed uncertain about whether to let him through, so she slipped past them to meet him, forestalling unnecessary conflict.

"Are you all right?" he demanded, gripping her arm briefly with his free hand as his eyes roamed over her, checking for injuries. His glance flicked back to Giles, emerging victorious from his recent encounter, and she realized that he must have seen the soldier attack her but not seen the outcome.

"I'm fine," she said quickly. "You?"

"Of course," he said absently, then lunged past her abruptly, his sword coming back red as he felled a soldier who had been running their way. "What's the goal here, Scarlett?" Jonan asked urgently, as if there had been no interruption. "How do we know who's won, and when? Because to my eye, it just seems like total chaos. It's as bad as the riot in the slave camp."

Looking around, she had to agree. It was pandemonium. The soldiers, whether in uniform or not, continued to make a concerted effort to get to the royals, but many of the towns-people were simply brawling with each other.

"Scanlon seemed happy with the progress, didn't he?" she muttered, half to herself. "But what was his plan? How did he hope to get a decisive outcome?"

Before she could do more than pose the question, Uncle Rupert raced past them, passing through the line of guards who parted respectfully for him. Scarlett saw him grasp his son by the shoulder, reassuring himself of Giles's safety in a rare display of sentiment. Then the older man's eyes flitted up to his brother on the balcony above, and she thought the concern on his face eased slightly.

Following his gaze, Scarlett let out a gasp. King Siloam still stood above the crowd, watching the commotion below, but he was no longer alone. The general stood by his side. And while that fact was clearly reassuring to Prince Rupert, it had the opposite effect on Scarlett, who suddenly understood Scanlon's plan. Of course the royal guards would not have hesitated to allow the general access to the king's receiving room back before the fighting broke out. Like Prince Rupert, they thought him trustworthy, and well-equipped to defend the king. He must have been hanging back out of sight of the courtyard all this time, probably speaking reassuringly to the oblivious king about how his soldiers would soon have the tumult under control. And the fact that he had now stepped forward to stand right beside the king seemed ominous. They had to get to him before he did anything permanent, but the guards surely wouldn't let her or Jonan in, and by the time she convinced Giles or her uncle and they ran through the castle to get there, it would probably be too late.

"Jonan," she yelled, her eyes still on the balcony. "The general is up there with the king!"

Jonan looked from her to the balcony and back. She met his eyes, her own expression apologetic, and knew that he didn't need her to explain in words what she was asking. He sighed.

"Why do I always boast about being a good climber?" he muttered to himself, but he didn't actually protest.

Sheathing his sword, he sprinted around the whipping post, mounting the steps up to the execution scaffold three at a time. Scarlett watched anxiously as he leaped from the deadly platform to the wall of the castle, grasping at a stone protrusion in the shape of a jaguar's head, the mouth open wide to let rainwater run out onto the flagstones below. He began to scale the wall with impressive speed. Scarlett was fairly certain she could have climbed it too, but she didn't think her dagger would be much good against the lethal sword the general always wore strapped to his side.

No one else seemed to have noticed Jonan's ascent, partially hidden behind the execution blade as he was. But the general's appearance must have been a pre-arranged signal, because a surge of soldiers suddenly rushed upon the small band of royals and their guards at the front of the courtyard. Scarlett found herself battling for her life, and was forced to tear her attention away from Jonan's progress.

Not at all sure that the royal guards would consider her protection a priority, she fought her way to Giles's side as quickly as possible. And it was well she did, for within a couple of minutes, the defenders had been forced into a tight knot, surrounded on all sides by attackers. For a moment they halted their forward press, and the hubbub seemed to lessen slightly.

"The king has shown he isn't willing to act to protect his people!" shouted someone from the crowd. The man wasn't in uniform, but there could be little doubt he was a soldier.

"We need a strong leader!" added another voice, and Scarlett wanted to roll her eyes. The words sounded rehearsed, like lines in a melodrama.

"How dare you!" cried King Siloam, suddenly reengaging with the situation. "I am your king! My people answer to me—I do not answer to them!"

"Well, perhaps you should!" The general's voice, strong and clear, seemed to ring out over the scene. The silver-haired veteran pulled out his sword with a metallic ring.

All eyes were now on the balcony. The general raised his weapon, and a sudden gasp ripped through the assembled watchers, whether from his actions or from the sight of the lithe figure vaulting over the railing of the balcony, it was impossible to tell.

King Siloam turned to his general with a cry that was echoed by his brother and nephew on the ground, all of them seeming to grasp the truth of the situation in the same moment. But the brazen attempt at regicide was thwarted, the general's sword unexpectedly meeting another blade as it swung toward the king. Jonan had reached his destination at last, and he threw himself between the two men, blade raised.

The shock of the crowd was palpable as Jonan not only resisted the attack, but pressed the much older and more experienced fighter backward. Only Scarlett was not surprised at the rush of power and energy that fueled Jonan's swordplay. If ever Jonan had sacrificed his own interests, it was now, when he put his very life on the line for the sake of the country that had despised and abused him, to defend the childish king who had only that morning ordered his execution.

Jonan's strength was more than enough to beat off the other man's attacks, but he still couldn't match the general for swordsmanship. His efforts to get under the man's guard were in vain. But the general, clearly astonished to the point of incredulity by Jonan's unexpected skill, was not paying enough attention to his surroundings as he was forced continually backward.

Jonan pressed the general toward the balcony's edge, and he stepped back one time too many in his efforts to avoid the younger man's ferocious lunges. The watching crowd below realized the inevitable a moment before the general did, and his desperate attempts to regain his balance were in vain. To the sound of gasps and screams, he toppled backward off the balcony, landing on the steps up to the execution scaffold with a sickening crunch. For a moment there was a hush, then shouts rent the air.

"Treason!"

"He's dead!"

"Get the Kyonan!"

The courtyard was suddenly more chaotic than ever, as everyone shouted out according to their own agendas, and no one quite knew what to do. The ring of soldiers surrounding Scarlett and the others wavered, unsure how to respond to this unexpected loss of their leader. At that propitious moment, a fresh squadron of royal guards emerged from the castle and sped toward the group in good order. Civilians scattered before them, and after a moment of hesitation, the soldiers surrounding the royals broke ranks and fled, the guards pursuing them into the streets.

All this Scarlett took in only vaguely, her eyes fixed on Jonan, who was peering down at the body of his fallen adversary. He seemed unsure what to do himself, now that the coup was over.

As she watched, she saw a couple of royal guards race onto the balcony. They bustled their sovereign out of sight, then returned and attempted to seize Jonan. He raised his sword, his expression hard, and Scarlett gave an involuntary cry of alarm. She had seen enough.

CHAPTER FIFTEEN

"Scarlett, where are you going?!"

She ignored Giles's shout, racing toward the entrance of the castle, dimly aware that someone was following her. As she sped through the familiar hallways, heading for the royal wing, she realized that both Giles and Uncle Rupert were accompanying her. It was fortunate that they were, because she would never have been admitted to the king's rooms without a fight. They, however, passed through the watching guards unhindered, Giles bringing Scarlett in his wake.

The guards inside were still tussling with Jonan, who was now in the room rather than out on the balcony, but Scarlett was relieved to see no sign of bloodshed. The door to the balcony remained wide open, and the din from outside had considerably lessened.

"Stop," said Prince Rupert commandingly, and the guards hesitated. He looked at his brother. "Siloam, surely you're not ordering this boy to be apprehended?"

"What?" The king seemed to come back to reality with an effort, clearly still dazed from his recent shock. He looked around and took in the scene before him. "No, of course not. Leave the Kyonan be."

The guards stepped back instantly, and Jonan smoothed his ruffled tunic aggressively, glaring at them.

Scarlett threw herself forward, disregarding the exalted company. Jonan put his free arm around her and they shared a brief embrace before she stepped back. She noticed that with his other hand he maintained his grip on his sword, his eyes still sweeping the room warily. Looking around, she could understand why. The noise from the courtyard had all but ceased—the riot really did seem to be over. But inside the room, the tension remained thick. Everyone was staring at Jonan, and while their expressions were more stunned than unfriendly, it was still unnerving.

Uncle Rupert was the first to speak, clearing his throat uncomfortably. "It seems that thanks are in order. We are in your debt. Both of you." His eyes crossed to Scarlett and she raised her eyebrows, not quite ready to let him off the hook. She was certain from his discomfited expression that he was remembering their fruitless conversation earlier that morning.

"If I'm honest, I did it more for Scarlett than for you, Your Highness," said Jonan. The laugh in his voice seemed to be directed at himself and somehow robbed the speech of insolence. "But I'm happy to be of service." He took in the sober faces all around him and seemed unable to resist a cheeky grin. "It almost makes it worth not chopping my head off, doesn't it?"

Scarlett gave a choked sound, somewhere between a laugh and a snort. She gripped Jonan's hand tightly, whether to communicate solidarity or restraint she wasn't entirely sure.

"We are definitely in your debt," echoed Giles, "and I'm man enough to own it when I'm wrong." He strode forward and offered his hand. After a moment of hesitation, Jonan put his sword away and returned the grasp. "I can admit that you had little enough reason to help us, Jonan. I was obviously mistaken about you," said Giles handsomely, and Scarlett beamed at her cousin.

"No harm done," said Jonan cheerfully, his generous words contradicted by the bruises still blooming across his face. "But when you come and visit us in Kyona, you owe me at least one night in King Calinnae's dungeons."

Prince Rupert narrowed his eyes, but Giles just laughed. "It sounds fair."

"And," added Jonan, his tone growing more serious. "I would be grateful if you'd stop trying to separate me and my wife, because she did marry me by choice, you know."

Giles grimaced in acknowledgment of the criticism, but it was King Siloam who unexpectedly answered.

"Of course there will be no more talk of separating you! You must both stay here in Nohl." He turned to Jonan, his face unusually enthusiastic. "You saved my life, after all! You must be rewarded. The general himself—I can hardly believe it. He will have to be replaced, and soon." The king brightened, as if struck by a sudden idea. "You can replace him!"

Everyone in the room stared at King Siloam with blank faces, Giles even being betrayed into a sputtering sound that was not very princely.

"Brother!" protested Prince Rupert, sounding genuinely alarmed. "You must see that's impossible! You can't make a foreigner—a nineteen-year-old with no military experience—general!"

"Yes, I suppose that's true," admitted the king, and everyone breathed a sigh of relief. "How about my personal bodyguard?"

Uncle Rupert uttered a sound of protest, but Jonan jumped in before anyone could get too agitated.

"Thank you for the offer, Your Majesty, but I'm not at all

interested in staying in Balenol. I want to go home, without delay." He looked suddenly down at Scarlett. "That is—"

"Yes," she reassured him quickly. "I want to go home, too." She looked over at Giles. "I know we were supposed to stay a few weeks, but the visit has been more than eventful enough already."

He nodded. "Yes, as much as I hate to say it, I think it will be wisest for you not to linger. We can send a message to your captain to be ready tomorrow."

"The day after," suggested Jonan unexpectedly. Scarlett looked up at him in surprise, and he smiled at her. "I still haven't actually met your aunt, you know. Or Astor, or Roland." She started, realizing that he was right. "And," he added ruefully, "I wouldn't mind sleeping in a real bed for a couple of nights before going straight from dungeon to ship."

Giles winced, and even Uncle Rupert had the decency to look a bit uncomfortable at this comment.

"Of course," he said, with dignity. "You must want to rest and freshen up now. I'll have a servant show you to your room, and we would be delighted if you join the family for the midday meal."

Jonan blinked, apparently taken aback by the discovery that even a thwarted coup was not going to disrupt the meal schedule. Scarlett smiled to herself. *Welcome to life in the castle.*

"Thank you, Uncle, we will certainly join you," she said aloud. "But I know the way to our room, no need to summon a servant." She smiled up at Jonan. "It's been a long couple of days, and I want my husband to myself for half an hour."

She thought that her uncle and the king looked a bit scandalized by this announcement, but Giles just shook his head, smiling, as she dragged Jonan out of the room.

They walked in silence for a minute, Scarlett shooting side-long looks at Jonan. Her heart felt full to overflowing at the relief of being together again, but she also felt a pang of sympathy every time she looked at him. Now that they were alone, with no unfriendly eyes for him to look strong for, his weariness was evident in his every movement.

"What are you thinking about?" asked Scarlett quietly.

"Hmm?" he said, coming out of his reverie and smiling down at her. "I was just thinking that this must be the most eventful anniversary in history. Next year let's celebrate with a nice meal and an evening by the fire."

She laughed, leaning up to press a kiss on his very willing lips, delightfully unconcerned by the shocked glance of a servant who was hurrying past.

"It's a deal."

THE CHEERFUL GROUP that gathered on the dock to farewell the travelers formed a strong contrast to the scene of their arrival. Scarlett couldn't help but smile as she watched the antics of her two younger cousins, who were clearly trying to impress her husband. Roland in particular had taken quite a liking to Jonan on first meeting, and was showing every sign of budding hero-worship. Scarlett had a feeling that a Balenan state visit to Kyona would not be too far off, and if she knew anything about it, Roland would be sure to cajole his way onto the delegation.

Even more pleasant was the sight of Aunt Mariska saying an affectionate goodbye to Jonan. A day and a half was obviously not long enough to really get to know one another, but Aunt Mariska had embraced Jonan warmly at first meeting. And Jonan, with a generosity Scarlett really thought was angelic, had responded readily, with no hint of reproach for his original, violent reception. She knew they had both done it out of love for her more than anything, but that didn't lessen the satisfaction. On the contrary, she felt richer than she ever had.

"Don't take this the wrong way, but I'll be relieved when you take your Kyonan firebrand back home. And not just because the city is still a tinderbox."

Scarlett turned to see Giles beside her. She couldn't help but smile as her eyes followed the direction of his gaze. He obviously didn't find Astor and Roland's merriment as amusing as she did.

"But everyone is getting on so well," she said innocently.

He shot her a look. "A little too well. I'm not sure he's a good influence on my brothers. This morning I heard Roland asking Astor whether he thinks a blade would give him as good a scar on his face as Jonan got from the whip."

Scarlett laughed in spite of herself. "He got more than one scar out of that episode," she said, smiling at the old joke. But her thoughts quickly turned serious again. "Speaking of brothers, you promised to tell me the latest news about mine."

Giles sighed. "It's nothing good, I'm afraid. It seems he's going to get away without consequences after all."

"What?!" Scarlett protested. "He was behind it, Giles, I know with absolute certainty! I heard him myself."

"I know," said Giles quickly. "And I believe you. And Father does too. But it's not up to us. And there's no evidence, other than your word, and Jonan's. And don't take offense, but that's just not considered trustworthy as far as the court is concerned. Scanlon was more careful than you think. I know he seemed careless in front of you, but I'm afraid he was entirely right that your word couldn't do him any harm. He played his hand well. All the blame is falling on the general, who is conveniently not able to refute any of it, since Jonan pushed him off a balcony. Not that I'm complaining," Giles hastened to add as Scarlett opened her mouth to protest. "My point is just that there's nothing concrete to prove that Scanlon had anything to do with it."

"I don't like it Giles," said Scarlett, uneasy. "He's not finished making mischief, I'm sure of it."

"I'm sure he'd like to cause trouble," agreed Giles. "But he won't get the opportunity. We may not be able to punish him for what he did, but you can be sure he'll never be trusted again, by anyone in my family. And we'll make very sure he doesn't get access to the king."

Scarlett frowned. It didn't satisfy her, but it was something, she supposed. And it wasn't her problem after all. She would be far away in Kyona, and surely Scanlon would never dare to venture there.

"You two look very serious," Jonan said, joining them. "I hope nothing's amiss. If you tell me that king of yours has changed his mind again, I'm going to fight this time. I've had enough of your dungeons to last me a lifetime."

"I think now you're more in danger of being conscripted into his military than thrown into his dungeons," answered Scarlett in amusement. "But don't worry, I'll spring you if necessary, even if I have to fight every royal here."

"Now I've seen you both in action, I wouldn't dare defy you," joked Giles. He offered Jonan his hand. "I am sorry, for all of it. And I'm glad things worked out as they did."

"Glad my head is traveling back to Kyona still attached to my body, you mean?" asked Jonan with a grin as he shook the offered hand. "Well, so am I. And I do hope you'll visit us. Because it would be nice to get to know Scarlett's family better, or at least some of her family. You'll have to come to us next time, because—no offense—I don't think we'll be back anytime soon." He looked around and lowered his voice conspiratorially. "Maybe when you're king—by then you'll have had time to sort all this chaos out."

"Time to go I think," said Scarlett dryly. "Before you get arrested for treason, again."

Scarlett was still standing on the deck half an hour later, as the port of Nohl grew small, and the figures of her family were no longer visible. Jonan had gone below when they first pushed off, but she heard his firm step behind her now. She didn't turn, but suddenly she felt something slip around her throat, Jonan's familiar hands securing a clasp at the back of her neck.

"Happy anniversary—here's your present at last," he said cheerfully.

She looked down, surprised. She had forgotten all about his casual mention of a gift. She lifted the delicate chain with her fingers, admiring the beautifully wrought metal, silver and gold entwining to form the chain. She stared for a moment at the pendant dangling from the end of it.

"Sorry it's late," said Jonan. "But I needed to fix it—it was missing something. I'll admit, Giles helped me out."

For a long moment, Scarlett said nothing, just turning it over in her fingers. The central pendant was a beautifully designed flower, wrought in silver with a white gem glinting in its center. She recognized it as a dianmon, a flower that grew only in Kyona's mountains and was often used as an emblem for the kingdom. It was evident that this flower had been the original focus of the necklace. But added on either side of the white flower were two identical flowers wrought in gold, made red by the gems that studded them. She had no difficulty identifying the hibiscus that grew in abundance in the jungle surrounding Nohl.

She felt tears pricking her eyes as she turned to look up at her husband over her shoulder. "It's beautiful," she said softly. "Thank you."

He put his arms around her from behind, drawing her back against him as he joined her in looking out over the railing at the swiftly receding shoreline.

"You're welcome," he said, his voice equally soft.

For a minute there was silence, then Jonan spoke again. "You looked very pensive, standing here all alone, looking at the ocean. What was weighing on your mind, sweetheart?"

Scarlett smiled at the term of endearment and the softness of Jonan's question, a rare show of tenderness from her usually energetic husband.

"You know what?" she said. "Nothing at all. I was just feeling happy to be going home."

Thank you for reading *Captive's Return*. I hope you enjoyed the quick escape into Scarlett's world. I would be so grateful if you would consider leaving a review on Amazon—it would really make a difference!

If you want to find out what the next generation of Kyonans get up to, check out *Legacy of the Curse*, the fourth installment of the Kyona Chronicles, where more adventure, fantasy, mystery, and romance await.

Join up to my mailing list at deborahgracewhite.com to be kept up to date on new releases, specials, and giveaways, such as bonus chapters. You will also receive *Dragon's Sight*, an 8,000 word prequel to the series, told from Elddreki's perspective.

Again, thanks for entering the world of the Kyona Chronicles! I hope to see you back again.

ACKNOWLEDGMENTS

After I finished writing Book Two, I found myself wondering about the trip back to Balenol that Scarlett mentioned in the epilogue. I thought there was a story to be told, and I liked the idea of spending some time in Scarlett's head. What started as a short story somehow became a whole novella.

As always, making that happen involved the support of many people. My first thank you goes to my husband Ray, my alpha reader, my cheer squad, and the reason I know firsthand that the romance doesn't end once you tie the knot!

A big thank you as well to my beta readers: Mum, Dad, Andrew, Adrian, Tamara, and Cherilyn. You guys are the best. As usual, a big thanks to Dad for your developmental and copy editing, to Mum for your line editing, and to Dad and Mel for your help with publication and release.

Karri, your cover is amazing as always, thanks for being patient as I scrawled through dozens of models in ballgowns. Rebecca, the map still blows me away every time I look at it.

To you, the reader, thank you for giving me the privilege of being an author.

And most importantly, to God, who brings light into the darkest of places.

ABOUT THE AUTHOR

I've been a reader since I can remember, growing up on a wide range of books, from classic literature to light-hearted romps. The love of reading has traveled with me unchanged across multiple  continents, and carried me from my own childhood all the way to having children of my own.

But if reading is like looking through a window into a magical and beautiful world, beginning to write my own stories was like discovering that I could open that window and climb right out into fantasyland.

I cannot believe how privileged I am to actually be living that childhood dream and publishing my own novels. I do so from my hometown of Adelaide, Australia, where I live with my husband and our two, soon to be three, little munchkins.

I've never outgrown my love of young adult stories, and my first series, the Kyona Chronicles, is a young adult fantasy series of four novels and two novellas.

Feel free to email me at deborah@deborahgracewhite.com and introduce yourself! Or subscribe to my mailing list at deborahgracewhite.com for free giveaways, sales, and updates.

9 781925 898255